SWING IN THE HOUSE

Swing in the House

AND OTHER STORIES

Anita Anand

ESPLANADE
Books

THE FICTION SERIES AT VÉHICULE PRESS

Published with the generous assistance of the Canada Council for the Arts, the Canada Book Fund of the Department of Canadian Heritage, and the Société de développement des entreprises culturelles du Québec (SODEC).

Esplanade series editor: Dimitri Nasrallah
Cover design: David Drummond
Typeset in Minion and Mrs Eaves by Simon Garamond
Printed by Marquis Printing Inc.

LIBRARY AND ARCHIVES CANADA CATALOGUING IN PUBLICATION

Anand, Anita, author
Swing in the house : and other stories / Anita Anand.

Issued in print and electronic formats.
ISBN 978-1-55065-398-4 (pbk.). – ISBN 978-1-55065-407-3 (epub)

1. Title.

PS8601.N28S95 2014   C813'.6   C2014-908333-5   C2014-908334-3

Published by Véhicule Press, Montréal, Québec, Canada
www.vehiculepress.com

Distribution in Canada by LitDistCo
www.litdistco.ca

Distributed in the U.S. by Independent Publishers Group
www.ipgbook.com

Printed in Canada

à Frédéric:

me voilà, encore ébahie

Contents

What I Really Did

You say you want to know what we did on our summer vacation, but do you really want to know? Why would you ask teenagers this question? You know that for most of our supposed vacation I was taking remedial math. You don't know about the last two weeks. All right.

On the last day of August I travelled to Barcelona with my parents. My mother had an obsession with mosaics. The trip was a present from my dad to my mom. They brought me along because what else were they supposed to do with a thirteen-year-old girl? It was too late to send me to camp. The hotel was a three-star, four-storey job. Our room had a double bed and a cot in the corner for me. The comforters were plush and orange. Not super exciting, although my mother kept exclaiming to my father how clean everything was, as if she had been expecting to be living in filth for two weeks.

The two of them went off every day to look at tiles. I always pretended to be sleeping in the morning when they set off, so after trying to wake me up a few times they would leave me alone. As soon as they left, I would raid my mother's cosmetic bag, put on loads of makeup, a long t-shirt but no shorts, just underwear, and flip-flops, and run to the plaza by the magazine stores, the plaza they didn't know about, where the other *putas* stood around chewing gum and tottering on their high heels. I say "other" but I was not really a prostitute, just a wannabe, just a kid travelling with her parents hoping something would happen to her.

I never actually got picked up. I don't think it was because I was too young. The makeup made me look almost ten years older, I swear. Maybe it was the flip-flops.

However, on the last day, I went to another plaza where artisans were selling their stuff and where a group of Peruvian buskers were playing. I spoke to a beautiful man who was selling cheap jewellery, and to my relief he understood my Spanish, whereas none of the locals could. This was because Jorge was Peruvian, and Mr. Cortes teaches us South American, not European Spanish. I joked that I wanted to buy some jewellery but had no money, so would he just give me some? He picked a necklace off its hook. It consisted of a pewter chain with a long cross made out of wood, crudely painted green and studded with tiny tiles. He put it around my neck. Then he asked me if I wanted to go somewhere with him.

Jorge was tall, had very dark skin, very long straight black hair, and stunning green eyes that were much more like jewels than anything he was selling. He packed his stuff in a little wooden case, took my hand and led me out of the square. I thought of saying "I am thirteen" but the words didn't come out. We went in a little red door and then up a set of narrow stairs, into a small, barely furnished apartment. We went into his bedroom. There was a mattress on the floor and a light bulb hanging from the ceiling. He motioned to me to lie down. I asked him to tell me about where he was from, but he was one of those people who looks really artistic but does not have an imagination or a flair for words. He just said he was from Peru and that he was an Indian. I asked him to tell me about his family and he just snorted. I gave up and let him kiss me and pull up my shirt and kiss my breasts. He took his jeans off and started to pull off his underwear and I asked him about condoms. He said he would be careful.

My Canadian education asserted itself.

"Necissita usar un condom," I repeated several times until he gave up and put his pants back on. He lay on his back, smiled at the ceiling and shook his head, sighed, smiled at me, shrugged, and told me I was killing him, that he was in agony. He kept his hand on his crotch and I looked at it curiously. I hadn't actually ever seen an erection before, and wished I had been paying more attention when he was in his underpants. I asked him if he wanted his necklace back and he just laughed and asked me how old I was. I turned onto my stomach and put my head in the pillow so that he couldn't see me blush.

After a while he said he had to go run some errands. Did I feel like waiting for him? I said it depended on what time it was. He laughed at that too and asked why. He said life was too short to worry about what time it was. I told him that he was right and that it didn't matter. I told him that because I couldn't very well say it was because I had to be back at the hotel room ten minutes before my parents returned so that I could wash my face and put some pants on.

He got up and went down the stairs and out the door. About a minute later, I went out too. Suddenly I realized I was lost. I hadn't paid attention to how we had gotten here from the plaza. I ran a few blocks to make sure I wouldn't run into him, and just started walking any which way. The air was starting to get sticky and smell like meat. After what seemed like an hour I heard Peruvian flutes and ran towards them. I froze as I spotted my parents walking hand in hand, their backs to me. I ran in the other direction for several blocks and found myself back at the end of Jorge's street. Jorge was knocking on his own door. He was holding a small white paper bag with a picture of a green cross.

Before he could turn and notice me I flew back the way I had come, and miraculously found myself back in the street of our hotel. Sitting on a bench by the door were a Turkish couple my parents and I had met in the elevator. They squinted at me curiously but did not seem to recognize me. I ran into the hotel, washed my face in the bathroom on the mezzanine, and took the fire escape up to our room. I crossed my fingers and prayed that my parents hadn't come back yet. I turned the key in the lock and crept inside.

They didn't notice I wasn't wearing pants. What they noticed was the necklace.

"That's beautiful," my mother said.

"You should have let us buy that for you, honey," my father said. "We've been looking for something for you. We feel so bad that you've been left on your own so much."

"How much did you pay for that?" my mother asked, opening her purse.

Swing in the House

One day, Julie came home from a doctor's appointment to find Mike washing his hair in the sink. He looked up at her warily.

"It's easier to clean up," he said by way of an explanation before ducking under the tap again.

What was he talking about? Curious, Julie peeked into the sink: mixed with the white foam from the shampoo were heavy purple drops. These formed muddy brown rivulets that cascaded down the white enamel.

She was dumbfounded. For a few minutes, she watched him. *Who is this man?*

"I didn't know you dyed your hair," she said.

"Well, I'm stopping now. Too bloody messy."

"What colour is your hair naturally?" Julie asked.

"Oh, I don't know. Reddish brown, I guess."

"Well, that's a nice colour." She remembered the school photo on the mantelpiece at his parents' house. Of course, it made sense. Red-haired little boys didn't suddenly turn completely raven-haired.

Almost a year they had been married. And he still had secrets.

Mike snorted, misunderstanding the disappointment in her voice.

"I can't take it anymore," he said. "You're winning, okay? It's a war of attrition, and you're winning."

* * *

Patty was talking about her pregnancy, about all the vitamins and examinations and tests. One test had a woman's name. Eliza.

"What's that?" Julie asked.

"An AIDS test. Didn't you have one?" Patty said. She and her husband Lionel had dropped in with their six-month-old daughter, Angeline. Now the two couples sat across from each other on the rolled-out futon, their babies asleep in the middle. It was mid-December, 1989. Outside, thick snow was falling over Montreal.

"Well, they *made* me have one," complained Patty. "It was negative, of course."

"Funny. How come they never asked me to?"

"Come on. You know. Look at your husband," Lionel said, laughing.

Mike and Julie looked at each other, baffled.

"What?" they said together.

"He's white," Lionel said. "*I'm* black. And *they're* really racist."

Lionel and Patty both laughed, as if this was uproariously funny. Julie looked at Lionel's inky black face, his startling white grin, then at Mike, pink with embarrassment, looking very privileged, English, and unattractive, like a member of the Royal Family. She felt a protective ache in her chest.

Baby Angeline woke up then, with a howl of protest.

The two couples lived around the corner from each other on the Plateau Mont-Royal. When Patty and Lionel left with Angeline, Julie and Mike stood at the door and waved. The fresh air felt good after hours spent in their overheated four-and-a-half. Huge snowflakes, the size of small birds, fell from the sky. Julie hadn't slept well and her nerves were raw. She had been having trouble following the conversation.

Many things had happened in the last month: the Berlin Wall had come down. Julie had given birth to a son. What she felt for him was beyond anything she had ever experienced before. Eleven women had been gunned down at a university campus a few kilometres away. In retaliation for the university massacre, a woman had threatened the male babies in the maternity wards of all the hospitals in Montreal. Julie thought she might be cracking up, or that her marriage was breaking up; she wasn't sure which. She wasn't sure when it had actually started. It seemed to her that she and Mike hadn't spoken to each other in a long time. He surprised her by speaking to her now.

"Actually," Mike said, as he closed the door. "I've had an AIDS test."

Paul began to stir. Julie picked him up and laid him across her chest. Eyes still closed, his tiny hand waved like a sea frond and brushed hers. She held his fingers and thought how fragile he looked. *Don't rock the boat.* An expression she had taught Lionel, who was from Zaire. Also, *walking on ice. Tread carefully.* Her mind was full of fortune-cookie warnings. So she said simply, in an even voice, "Why?"

"Well, you were pregnant. I thought I should."

"But you said nothing happened. You said you only kissed Ishl."

"Oh, please drop it. It's over. Please, for him."

That is who the AIDS test was for. Of course. For the baby. Drop it. Let sleeping dogs lie.

Mike turned on the TV. On the news, students in the Czech Republic were about to honour the twentieth anniversary of the death of a man who had set himself on fire to protest the Soviet occupation. Or more precisely, the reporter was saying, the demoralization caused by the occupation. Julie stood behind the couch and watched her husband watch TV.

Did they love each other? Had they ever? Was it just that what they felt for their son made their feelings for each other pale in comparison? Watching her son sleep, she thought the word *love* didn't begin to describe her feelings and Mike's for this new perfect being they had somehow thoughtlessly conjured up out of nothing.

15

A new word was needed, a verb that meant *I would immolate myself for you.*

Julie woke up the next morning with a headache, thinking she had better check the basement, wondering how to get there, why she hadn't noticed any stairs, realizing with great relief that they didn't have a basement, that she had only been dreaming.

She had dreamt that Mike hid Ishl in the basement, fucking her more often than he did her. That she had chased her out once, but would probably have to do it regularly, as Ishl just laughed at all the cruel things she said to her. She thought of telling Mike about the dream, but knew that he would probably just clam up. Then she would fly into a rage, and he would say something contemptuous about monogamy and the middle classes, which he pronounced *clawses*. A sentence seemed to click on and off in her brain like a neon sign, announcing the truth, the answer: she and Mike were not compatible. But she wasn't ready to let that brittle insight penetrate her heart.

Many people had observed Julie and Mike's first meeting. He was obnoxiously handsome and knew it. You could see it in his eyes as he rose from his chair and introduced himself to her at the party. A glass of vodka in one hand. Absolut suave. Mid-Atlantic accent. He had her at hel-looo, all her friends said. The heady scent of linden trees in Daniella's garden, the orange glow of the tealights, the way he kept making her smile with his smile. All seemed to emanate from his almost cartoonish good looks. Thick black hair, fine features, muscular build. A Saturday-morning superhero, a fairytale prince, a man modelling boxer shorts in a catalogue.

She dropped by where he worked, saying she had being doing an errand in the neighbourhood. Mike sat in his studio and bragged about his soundproof walls. Twelve hours a day he sat there composing advertising jingles. He did that with the help of various beeping, blinking electronic devices; occasionally he took his clarinet out of the case tucked away at his feet. *Sometimes* he took weekends off. He derived equal pleasure, he told her warningly, from his work and from his solitude. He told her that he had once found a similar sort of happiness on a trip to Burma.

"A cliché, really," he said, though he didn't seem embarrassed. "You know, motorbike, incognito, wind in your hair, destination undecided."

His hair had the thickness and gloss of the coat of a wild animal. She wanted to grab it in her hands. She didn't like the idea of him on that motorbike. She imagined him carelessly careening around a precipice, being thrown off and flying through the air. What would happen to that pretty face of his?

He would be safer with her, she decided.

Their first night together, as if sensing danger, he told her he didn't want to get involved.

"I know," she said, "That's all right."

But somehow she got pregnant and he was the one who decided they had to get married. Her terror, her feeling of utter stupidity, the lost look on her face, seemed to seduce him completely, loins *and* heart, maybe for the first time. Anyone could have told them that it wouldn't last very long.

ATTRITION n.1. the act of wearing away or the state of being worn away, as by friction 2. Constant wearing down to weaken or destroy (often in the phrase war of attrition) 3. Geography – the grinding down of rock particles by friction during transportation by water, wind or ice. Compare abrasion 4. Theol. Sorrow for sin arising from fear of damnation, esp. as contrasted with contrition, which arises purely from love of God (C14: from Late Latin attrition a rubbing against something, from Latin *atterere*, to weaken, from *terere* to rub.)

"Jesus," said Mike. "You really should read more."

"I am only twenty-two," Julie said, though she realized it was a weak argument; Mike was four years older. She realized that what she didn't understand wasn't the word. It was what he was trying to say.

They had gotten on that train again, the one that could only lead to another fight that would leave her confused. She put her coat on, packed baby Paul in the snuggly and walked to Patty and Lionel's. She tried to take her mind off things by admiring the beauty of her neighbourhood: wrought-iron staircases, pretty, old-style masonry, funkily painted walk-up duplexes and triplexes. She walked up the winding staircase of her friends' apartment, knocked on the door and then just opened it, as was their arrangement.

Patty was making a cake. She told Julie the story of her sister's life. Three kids and an abusive alcoholic husband. He called the kids "shits," raped her, told her she was ugly, drove like a madman.

"Why do you think he tells her she is ugly?" Julie asked.

"Oh, that's the least horrible of his insults."

"What else does he say?" Julie asked, horrified and fascinated.

"Every day he comes up with something that will hurt her more."

"Why? What has she done to him?"

"Ishl has a theory…"

"Oh yeah?" Julie said. She always kept her voice casual and her face neutral at the mention of that name; she was too proud to tell anyone of her suspicions. To most people, Ishl was a radical lesbian feminist set painter with entertaining takes on things. To Julie, she was a dangerous, though invisible, bisexual threat. She never saw Ishl, except at the occasional party, but she constantly felt her.

"Yeah… it's that… she refuses to leave."

"She refuses to leave?" Julie said, a slight ache developing in her chest.

"Yes, Ishl thinks that's what he does it for. He wants to force her to leave. Ishl calls it a war of attrition."

They use the same words. Julie forced herself to shrug, to breathe normally. There was a picture in her head of Mike and Ishl, standing close together at a party at the anarchist theatre where Ishl worked. Ishl had a radical, platinum haircut, an eyebrow piercing, a nose ring and several earrings. When Julie had come up to them, she heard Ishl whisper, "Oh, shit, here she is", before she slid away, the back of her head like a light as she slipped through the knots of people. Julie wondered if the weekends when Mike had to be alone meant alone with *her*.

He didn't disappear very much anymore. He stayed home now. But he seemed utterly miserable.

Attrition. She had known it was about rubbing, but thought it had something to do with sex. People rubbing each other the wrong way, wearing each other down with too much friction, too much grinding. In her heart, she still felt that Mike needed her. He needed her to keep him moored.

Snowy February morning. Julie stood next to Mike's chair as he watched videotaped footage of hockey players hurting one another. The couple communicated without speaking.

"But it's so beautiful outside," Julie pleaded in her head. "It's all sparkling white and magical. Please come outside and make snow angels with us."

"I don't understand why there's a problem," Mike seemed to reply, staring at the screen. "I'll stay inside and be happy, and you can go outside and be happy. I won't judge or try to stop you for wanting to go outside in subzero temperatures. Ergo, you have no right to put down what I am interested in. We're two separate beings. Do whatever. Individual needs."

"I'm unbearably lonely," she thought as she zipped Paul in his snowsuit and put him inside her coat. "And so are you."

As soon as she stepped outside, the clouds in her head began to dissipate. A bright yellow sun shone in the beautiful clear morning, like in a child's drawing. The fresh snow met her boots with a satisfying crunch. She walked aimlessly for a time, then turned towards home. When she felt the vague sadness return, she headed to Patty and Lionel's. She tried the door; it was locked.

She was about to turn and go down the steps when Lionel

19

appeared, smiling. He greeted baby Paul, who beamed back at him. Through the open door she glimpsed Patty at the kitchen table. She was in tears. *A lover's spat? Are they like us?* She wondered what to say, how to apologize for this intrusion, but Lionel, having followed her gaze, surprised her by inviting her in. Paul gurgled and cooed.

Lionel insisted, waving his arms expansively. "You see, your boy likes it here."

Patty looked up at Julie, still crying, apparently unembarrassed.

"She's tired," Lionel said, and put his arm around her. Patty nestled into him, closed her eyes and smiled.

Their apartment was dingier than Julie and Mike's, with a slanting floor and a smell of damp wood, but they had painted the walls orange and gold and decorated them with large black and white photographs of their naked bodies, black and white, entangled together. The kitchen looked completely decrepit; the linoleum on the counters was peeling and turning brown for some reason; the sink, full of dirty dishes, had rust around the taps. Cheerful African music was playing on a cassette recorder on top of the fridge. The room smelt of fruit and herbal tea.

They told Julie how Angeline cried virtually all night, how they couldn't figure out what was wrong with her.

"She's just a nasty baby," Lionel said, his accent heavy and humorous on "nasty." He put a cup of tea in front of Patty, and kissed her on the top of her head.

Patty declined the tea and, despite her exhaustion, pulled herself up from her chair, put her coat on and came out for a walk. Once outside, she complained bitterly about her baby daughter, and told Julie she was obscenely lucky that Paul slept through the night. But Julie remembered the warmth of their kitchen, Lionel's tenderness, and how he had convinced her to leave him with the baby for a while. She felt a rush of envy, quickly followed by guilt. *Be happy for your friends*, she told herself. She knew that Lionel hadn't had an audition for a long time, and that the couple survived on welfare and the occasional decorating job.

Winter went by. The weather warmed up. An unusually warm late May evening, the kind of evening which always felt exciting and full of promise in Montreal. The leaves were barely on the trees, but the air was hot and sultry. People shed their jackets, walked around the Plateau soaking up the atmosphere. Jazz floated out from cafés and bars. On a sudden impulse, Lionel and Patty decided to blow their welfare cheque. They left Angeline with Julie and Mike while they went to a restaurant three blocks away. Julie estimated that Mike's job paid about five times as much as their friends earned under the table or received through government supplements at any given time. She longed to go out with them; she could have picked up the tab. The babies could have slept in their strollers. Well, maybe not Angeline, she reflected. She told herself firmly that she was happy to babysit for them, and when they didn't come back when they were supposed to, didn't mind stopping Angeline's hungry cries by putting her to her own breast. Angeline blinked with surprise for a few seconds, then sucked greedily.

"I don't think Patty nurses her anymore, does she?" said Mike.

"I know, but she didn't leave us a bottle for her." Julie wiped the sweat from Angeline's brow.

"If you ask me, she *should* nurse her. She could lose a little weight."

Julie wondered if Mike just felt like insulting her friend to score points against her, or was actually trying to reassure her that Patty was someone he would definitely not sleep with. Or maybe, it dawned on her, though not for the first time, he was just an asshole, and this was just… *honesty*. Honesty from an asshole. She pushed the thought away.

Julie told him that Patty had nursed her daughter three months, but that it seemed to make her sick. She didn't want to fight. Mike just snorted.

21

She looked down at the baby girl and combed her damp black curls with her fingers. There was a flush across her dark cheeks; her eyes were closed now. "I think I'd like a daughter too," she said in a playful voice.

Mike gave her a look that said, "Well, you've got your wish." or maybe, "Please leave me out of that wish of yours," or maybe just that he was going to bed. But as he rose to go to the bedroom, footsteps thumped up the stairs outside. He signaled to Julie to pull Angeline off her chest. By the time he opened the door to their friends, Mike and Julie both had wide fake smiles on their faces, as if they had nearly got caught doing something indecent.

Spring, summer, autumn. Late November now. Things Paul said: Baba, Ididit, Mama, Pappa, Daddy, and sometimes *ooo*. He pointed to things from his high chair and said, "Whazdis." At first, Julie would say, "Oh, that's your cup" or "That's a roll of tape" and he would go crazy, turn red and scream, until it dawned on her that he was asking for the thing in question. He liked to make Donald Duck sounds and to wrinkle his nose and sniff. He hated being dressed or changed. He was sociable, but sometimes scared by strangers. He was strikingly beautiful. She loved to hold him, breathing in his baby smell, watching his eyelids and his pout, the way his little thumbs curled under his fists, feel the warmth of his sleeping body. And she wished she could freeze the moment, and experience it again when she was better rested, when her head was clear. He wouldn't be small for long.

Paul was already one. The year had gone by so quickly, and he was already transformed from a listless little bundle with the tiniest fingers imaginable and the quietest kitten-like cry to a pudgy, mo- bile, boisterous little boy. He began walking. And carrying. He obsessively carried large objects—a stool, a coffee-table book, his father's winter coat—from one room to another. He reminded her of an ant dragging a breadcrumb across a sidewalk. This added a whole new dimension to housework. Julie now spent considerable chunks of her day looking for boots behind the bathtub, pots and pans under beds, recipe books in the toybox.

She told herself to cherish it all. She was all in pieces, and knew that part of what was tearing her apart was her envy of the people who had it all together.

The first of December. It was raining. The breeze from the window was soft. Paul asleep in Julie's arms. Julie reread the letter she had received from Patty, and considered its secret request. She gently shifted Paul to her left shoulder, removed the key from the envelope and stepped outside.

Around the corner on Duluth Street was a sad empty apartment. Patty had suddenly fled home to her parents in B.C. with Angeline. Lionel was in the hospital, suffering from a kidney dysfunction as well as some kind of mental breakdown.

That was what the doctors said. What Julie and Mike had seen: windows smashed; Lionel, suddenly very thin, his face contorted with rage, screaming, blaming Patty for everything that had gone wrong in his life; Lionel, lying on his side on the floor, weeping, arms wrapped tightly around his middle. Mike called an ambulance and, a few minutes later, after the screaming, the shattering and the sirens, the chaos turned into eerie silence.

The lock was stubborn now, as if the apartment was bracing itself for another attack. Julie finally managed to push the door open, and here came the smell: damp wood, garbage, sweat. There was broken glass everywhere, as if someone had swept it evenly between the rooms.

Julie went into the bedroom, the private, sacred room, feeling like an intruder despite the task she had been given. This was where Angeline was conceived; this was where Patty and Lionel had fought and made up and made love. Except Julie had never thought they really fought. She had assumed they were so much happier.

Still holding Paul with one arm, she followed Patty's instructions and located a shoebox full of letters. She sifted through them, these records of an unhappy marriage, and found the one that was particularly cruel, which Patty wanted to keep. As a memento, Julie supposed, as a kind of protection against remorse.

There were other things Patty wanted too: clothes, cassette tapes, photographs and knick-knacks. Her descriptions were well-detailed, her handwriting surprisingly even. Absence made the heart go harder. Still, Julie thought, she would not want to be in her shoes as she opened the package and the memories came flooding back again.

For some time afterwards, Julie didn't hear from her friend. Julie had worried dreams of Patty and her little daughter, fleeing an enraged Lionel. Standing on the street outside their apartment one night, Julie saw a light behind their curtains. Lionel had returned. Julie panicked; he would notice all the things that had gone, maybe realize who had taken them. One day when Julie was alone at home she heard a knock on the door. Peering around the living room window, she saw that, yes, it was him, and he looked irritated. Her heart suddenly felt like a wildly kicking baby, but in her chest. She dived behind the couch and hid.

Finally, at Christmas, a card came from B.C. A blurry picture of Patty and Angeline dressed in red and white coats. Patty was smiling happily; Angeline looked hot and smothered in her coat. Inside, Patty's large, enthusiastic handwriting: "Hi, you guys, sorry I haven't been in touch"—followed by instructions. Another package to be mailed out. Some of it from the apartment ("Lionel says he came by but that you were too scared to open the door—what were you afraid of?") and some from other friends' houses.

So Julie bundled up her son and went to visit Lionel. The old Lionel. Not so thin, and without a trace of rage. He smiled warmly, tickled Paul and made him squawk. He laughed as he informed Julie how funny she had looked, hiding behind the couch that day.

"Hey, you're red!" he exclaimed, throwing back his head and laughing. Paul began to giggle. Julie was completely puzzled, and wondered if Lionel could see that too.

"So you're in touch with Patty?" she asked Lionel. "How is she doing?"

"Fine, fine. The only bad things she said is nobody write her letter. She keep sending some, get nothing back."

"But I've written her a lot," Julie protested.

He laughed again and told her she was right. "She said nobody write except you. I don't know what she complain about: nobody ever write to me from Zaire. For all I know, everybody dead." He laughed loudly at that.

He showed Julie a photograph he had just received: the same one, except it was in focus. He was upbeat, and unembarrassed, as if all couples went through something like this. After a few minutes Julie stood in the doorway with the box of paintbrushes Patty had asked for, Paul in an orange bag on her back, a hand-me-down gift from Lionel. No shadow on Lionel's face as he handed over this last article of his daughter's. He explained that he had given away all her clothes and toys to the Salvation Army.

"Would have give them to you, Paul, but your mama don't open the door, ha ha."

Julie walked through the snowy streets, Paul on her back, three boxes in her arms, and rang the doorbells of Patty's other friends. People she vaguely remembered opened their doors; they didn't recognize her, but when she explained why she had come they became warm and trusting, as if imitating Patty herself, and invariably showed her their Christmas cards. Patty and Angeline in red and white coats, in varying degrees of blurriness. At one house, the picture was in perfect focus. Julie glimpsed the message inside: "Dear dear Vanessa, I am sending you the best photograph." Vanessa had spiky blue hair and a lot of bangles and beads; Julie didn't recall meeting this one before.

All the way home, laden with baby and boxes, the words rankled. "Dear dear Vanessa, I am sending you the best photograph."

When Julie mailed Patty her parcels, she enclosed the bill for the postage.

April, 1991. Paul, throwing things from his high chair, named them as they landed. "Uh-oh," he said, with a comic look of insincere surprise. "Uh-oh, duh o-winge."

"Yes, uh-oh, the orange," Julie agreed. She picked the little crescent of tangerine up off the floor, scraped off the dark hair that had somehow wound itself around it, rinsed it off under the tap and popped it into her own mouth.

"Gone," she said, mimicking Paul's exaggerated shrug, shoulders almost touching her ears, arms outstretched, palms up. Or was Paul imitating *her*?

"Ya, gone," he agreed thoughtfully, before abruptly flipping his little cup of yogurt off the tray of his table. Peering down at the floor, he said, "Uh-oh, duh yogo."

The cup landed on its bottom, contents unspilled. She put it safely away on the kitchen counter. "Don't want it?" she asked. "Not hungry?"

Paul ignored the question. "Uh-oh, da poon!" he cried happily, his voice chiming with the sound of metal thunking to the floor. Yogourt from the spoon splashed onto her chair leg. She bent down to retrieve it, wiped up the mess with a wet cloth and—splat.

"Uh-oh, duh o-winge again!"

She extracted another bit of tangerine from inside her collar.

What she had hoped to do: put Paul—now seventeen months old, head sufficiently filled with words and images to sometimes amuse himself—into his high chair for ten minutes, and for these precious minutes let her mind slowly unclutter, maybe even have a little daydream.

"Uh-oh, Mummy, some mo o-winge!"

26

Realizing how much he was enjoying this game, she gave him back the spoon, and they played like this for another few minutes.

"Oh!"—always the same theatrical expression of bafflement in his high-pitched voice, on his cherubic face. "Uh-oh, mummy, the poon! Uh-oh, again!"

Julie put Paul in a pair of overalls and a t-shirt and got out the stroller. The day was overcast and mild, the air outside wonderfully soft and fresh after too many hours inside the stuffy apartment. She locked the door. Paul held her hand and they were carefully making their way down the winding iron staircase when next door a man, an unknown neighbour, came out of his apartment and locked his door.

But without the protection of a small child to slow his descent, the man, chic and anonymous in his flat cap and long coat, began to gallop down his identical staircase. Paul pulled on Julie's hand and stopped. He wanted to watch.

He was rewarded: sure enough, the man lost his footing, slid down the rest of the winding steps, and fell flat, face first, onto the sidewalk.

"Uh-oh," Paul squealed, thrilled, mock concern in his sing-song voice, "Uh-oh," he called out into the quiet street, clear as a bell. "Uh-oh, duh man."

Mortified, Julie let out a giggle.

The man rose, his back to the young mother and child, brushed himself off and silently continued down the street.

"Your climate is so bloody extreme," Mike said later that evening, having one of his periodic rants about the weather. They made his English accent come back. "I don't understand how anybody can live here. You go from freezing cold to boiling hot. You don't have spring. You have a few days when the snow melts and the trees, formerly bare, are suddenly lush."

"It's gorgeous," Julie protested.

"It's monstrous. It's not natural."

There was a silence while they both let his words sink in the way he meant them to. He liked this game of cleverly veiled accusations. Julie had trouble keeping up with him; she was never much good at games. She could only honestly tell him how she felt.

"In England," he continued, "we have spring. It's a beautiful, delicate, graceful transition. It has subtlety. Of course, you wouldn't get that."

"It rains." Her voice sounded whiny, even to herself. "And when it rains, the drops are bone-chilling. It's not happy weather."

They moved to B.C. She told herself it would be fine. For one thing, there would be distance between Mike and Ishl. Although she had no idea how much of a threat Ishl actually was, she was always there, behind Julie's thoughts, weighing down her dreams, as elusive and omnipresent as God, but with multiple piercings. And Patty was out there, living the isolated life of a single mother. Poor Patty. Maybe she could help her out.

Mike found work as a sound technician for a film studio in Richmond, a ten-minute drive from Vancouver. Julie began to work two part-time jobs. One consisted of teaching new immigrants "life skills," a job she had done full-time before Paul was born. The other consisted of finding host families for foreign students. They rented a house in an agricultural preserve in Richmond. There were willow trees, a small pond, a huge field of wild grass. Across the road, a cranberry field, where Sikhs in bright turbans stood knee-deep in dark crimson water. Julie reassured herself that Paul would be just as stimulated here as in a big city; the stimulants would just take different forms. When they went for walks, they counted the chickens, dogs, blue herons, ducks, horses, and even llamas, which their next-door neighbour mysteriously kept in his backyard.

Soon after they had settled in, Julie visited Patty, who lived in a similar area a half-hour away in White Rock. A home on her parents' property, a loft above a chicken house. She had decorated it in her vibrant style. Red floor, brightly patterned, contrasting cushions, an orange cat that sat and stared at them from the corner of the room.

Patty was in art school. She showed Julie some sketches she had done for a new self-portrait. Sweeping, sensual pencil strokes. Patty's face, but a little thinner and older and a great deal more wanton. Patty served Julie a cup of green tea and then settled her heavy body down on the red floor. On the wall behind her, looming over her: a life-sized portrait of a sharp-featured man in a rumpled shirt. Patty reached for the cat, but he whimpered and fled back to his corner.

Julie asked her what was new. Patty was coy; she beamed and shrugged.

"Who's that?'" Julie asked, pointing to the picture.

"Someone new, yes, not a boyfriend," but her eyes nevertheless shone. Like a little girl's. Or, it occurred to Julie, like a madwoman's. Julie wondered if she herself had had that look when she first met Mike. A woman in love.

Finally, Patty dropped her guard and began to talk. The guy in the painting was the opposite of the man Julie had helped her to leave in Montreal: that man had been a tall, beautiful African, an aspiring actor, had a very loud laugh and was prone to unpredictable rages.

"Do you remember?" Patty asked.

"Do I remember!" Julie exclaimed.

Patty told her that she was considering going back to Lionel. She said that she missed being a family, and she missed sleeping with him. "But so far, every time he says he's coming, he backs out at the last minute. But still..."

Julie shook her head at her friend, and mouthed, "No."

"Anyway, in the meantime, there's this guy from Berlin." She told Julie that the man who had posed for her was a set builder and aspiring film director with an intelligent, brooding way about him. He had followed his ex to Montreal, then come out to B.C. to recover from a broken heart.

"He actually married Ishl to stay in the country!" she added.

"What? He was with Ishl?"

"No, she just married him so that he could stay here. His girl-friend refused to. Ishl isn't into men, remember?"

Right, thought Julie. "You want to help him recover from his broken heart, is that it?" she asked as she glanced up at the picture. The subject seemed stiff and unwilling. Also, familiar. She looked back at Patty, who hugged her fat knees and sighed dreamily. Julie felt depressed. She made an excuse to leave.

Life went on. Work, kid, taciturn husband. Julie and Mike never left Paul with a babysitter to go out to supper or to a movie, but one Saturday, Julie arranged for him to have a play date so that she and Mike could go shopping for some new furniture for his room. As they were descending an escalator that day, a couple going up on the escalator beside them began to wave and shout excitedly at Mike.

"Hey, Mr. No-Forwarding-Address!" the man shouted. The woman yelled, "Mikey Smythe, you prick!" The man was tall and black-haired, with long black sideburns, the kind only the exceptionally beautiful can pull off. Mike reached for Julie's hand, surprising her. Paul did that, when he was nervous, and their hands, despite the difference in size, felt the same. The same warm stickiness. Julie watched her husband's face as the other couple scrambled off their escalator and ran around to theirs. Mike's lips were twitching.

"What are the chances?" The woman said, as she and the man caught up to them. She pronounced it *chawnces*.

"We are Andy and Billy, by the way," she said to Julie, giving no indication who was who. "But I expect you have heard all about us from Roo here." *Roo?* The woman slapped Mike softly on his right cheek.

"You know, I had a feeling you would end up here," the man said, and then added, "Wanker."

"In my defense, I was going to write to you…" Mike began.

"Is this your lovely wife?" the woman said. She touched Julie on the shoulder. "Lucky Mike. Lucky you too, though. Roo was my first crush, you know."

All Julie could get out of Mike on the way home was that they had been in a band together in England. No, no records. Just a high school thing. Not really music, more like Art, whatever that meant. Yes, he had known they lived here. No, he wasn't particularly keen on getting together with them.

"Was Andy *your* first crush?" Julie asked.

Mike stiffened. He didn't answer.

"Which one is Andy anyway?"

Silence.

"Have I got it wrong? Was *Billy* your first crush?"

But he had retreated into one of his mysterious funks. She cheered herself up by remembering how he had reached for her hand. She remembered the warmth of his fingers in hers, and also the need.

She knew she was never going to see those people again. If she wanted a social life, she would have to get it going by herself. The trouble was, Patty rarely wanted to get together. Julie gradually realized Patty was in love with the artist's life. Julie herself was in some inferior class of friend, she knew, someone not hip and artsy, and their relationship only consisted of occasional visits or phone calls. Work was all right; she led foreigners around town although she barely had a grasp of Vancouver at all. The glorious colours in which everyone had painted B.C. out east set her up for a letdown. The city seemed shabby, there was no street life, and that particular summer it rained every single day in July.

Julie did call Patty from a pay phone on her way home from work a few days in a row to try to coax her to come out on her birthday. She called her several times, maybe too many times, that week. Mike had encouraged her to. He didn't mind looking after Paul. Julie understood that he felt suffocated by her presence, by the routine they shared. Paul's innocent joy in discovering the world was contagious, and it mitigated his father's suffering, but somehow the effect didn't cross over into the realm of the relationship of his parents. Julie stuck to the belief that the relationship was still good for both of them. Where would they be without each other, without Paul? Mike had a restless streak; he was a hazard to himself. He would probably have quit working altogether if he hadn't had to support a family. He would be in Thailand. He would be addicted to drugs, she firmly believed, and probably have a few STDs by now.

Patty declined Julie's invitation again; recently she always seemed to be waiting to hear from her German friend. He would say he was coming by, then not show, or show up just as she was going to bed.

"I'm worried about you," Julie said.

"Yeah, I know. This isn't a great situation."

After a moment, Patty shocked Julie by asking if she thought she should "jump him" when or if he did eventually turn up. When Julie finally replied, her words were careless.

"Sure, why not? It couldn't hurt." She felt slightly depressed as she spoke.

She stalled going home. She walked through a park in the rain. A teenage boy had just taken a young husky off its leash, in defiance of the signs posted everywhere. The boy glanced at her and grinned as they watched the dog zip around and around in a big slanting circle, as if it had been waiting for this moment its whole life.

Julie finally got on a bus to go home. The bus was crowded. She paid her fare and, swinging along the overhanging handrail, made a brief attempt to pass through the tight knot of people at the front.

Suddenly, she came face to face with Patty's painting, her German friend. Their eyes met. Then his bounced away and returned to his book.

This is the only way for people with no real friends to meet people. By meeting other people's friends, by crazy coincidence. *No, why would it be him? Too much imagination,* she scolded herself. She studied him. Skinny, wearing too many layers for the weather.

A green denim jacket, two shirts, black jeans, a flat cap on his head. He had a pointy chin, sharp cheekbones, and startling light-blue, narrow eyes. He moved toward the back, his nose still in his book.

After a moment, she followed, and told herself that if the words on the cover of the book were German, her imagination had won.

They were.

"Excuse me," she said.

He looked up and smiled. A happy, trusting, inquiring, unsurprised smile.

"Yes?"

There was a pause during which they smiled at each other and she felt very pretty. There was also a vague flash of recognition. She tried to figure out what the feeling was, and decided it was that she was about to make a mistake again. A flash of recognition of the feeling before a big mistake.

"Are you Patty's friend?" she heard herself say.

"Yes," he answered, as if expecting the question. "And who are you?"

Julie mumbled her name, explained how she recognized him, and he said, very clipped, very German, that he seemed to recognize her too, and that Patty would be happy to hear that someone had recognized him from her painting. He didn't tell her his name. Then he rang the bell, excused himself and got off the bus.

Julie's heart sank. If he were interested, she told herself, he would have stayed on the bus. *Wait, interested?* She swore at herself, for everything. She listed the reasons in her head. For her apparent subconscious wish to deceive both her friend and her husband. For her stupidity at staying married to someone who clearly did not love her. She pushed *that* thought down. But, most of all, for her obvious unattractiveness. *If I were better-looking.* The thought accompanied her all the way home. She studied the posters on the bus advertising skin creams, hair dyes and holidays at beach resorts. *If I didn't have bags under my eyes, if my hair looked all right, if I looked good in a bikini.*

It finally stopped raining. The next morning, Julie was hanging clothes on the line outside when she heard Mike through the kitchen window, answering the phone.

"No, she never told me about it," he was saying. "Well, I don't know. Yeah, maybe we don't talk much."

"We're babysitting Angeline on Saturday," Mike announced as she came inside with the empty basket. "Patty needs a break."

Julie was surprised. She had given up calling Patty. She was happy that Patty had thought of her, and that she could help her with Angeline. Ever since the time she had nursed Angeline, the little girl had felt like a part of her family, as if she had managed to burrow under her skin.

"So you met this Max guy," Mike said. "Some crush of Patty's?"

"Oh, yeah, that's right," Julie said. She hesitated. She had gotten out of the habit of conversation with her husband since… since forever. He didn't seem particularly interested now. Or was he? Did he know Max through Ishl? Was he jealous? And of whom?

"It was embarrassing," she finally said. "For some reason the guy practically leapt off the bus when I went up to talk to him." A deep breath. "What did he tell Patty?"

"Oh, nothing much," Mike said, his face unreadable. But he went on to report what Patty had told him: Max nearly fainted when a beautiful woman with beautiful eyes got on his bus and told him she had recognized him from a painting.

"Oh, and he missed his stop," he added.

Angeline was almost six months older than Paul, but much taller, and with none of his babyishness. She watched primly as Paul splashed naked in his plastic wading pool in the backyard. She refused to even take off her sweater, although her brown face glistened with sweat.

"When's my mum coming back?" she asked.

"Tomorrow morning," Julie said.

"Are we having dessert tonight? I saw a cake."

Julie's heart sank. She had made the cake for her, remembering that her third birthday had just passed, but then Patty told her that Angeline had terrible skin rashes, and that she was trying to eliminate wheat from her diet to see if they would go away.

"It's not a very good cake," she told her. "I want to make you a different dessert. When this one is in bed"—she indicated Paul with her chin—"we'll go see what we can find."

Angeline's eyes lit up and she allowed herself a small, hopeful smile.

Later that night the little girl watched Julie gravely as she cut pieces of melon, banana and kiwi into a bowl. When she opened a container of strawberries, some kind of childish energy seemed to stir in her for the first time, and she hopped in the air, clapped and whooped for joy.

"Strawberries!" she sang happily, as she ran and hugged Julie around the waist.

A few days later, Julie, Mike and Paul returned home from work and daycare to find three messages on the answering machine. A record number.

Mumbling, "Oh shit," and then a small voice in the background whining, "I want to go to Julie's." Click. Then another message, this time an adult shouting her head off in the background, and a little girl saying, "Hello?" A third message. Shouting and crying. Nobody speaking into the phone.

Julie looked at Mike and for once they immediately agreed about something, albeit silently. After supper, Julie drove to Patty's parents' farm and parked next to the chicken coop. She stood next to the car, looking up into the window of Patty's place, patting the dog that had rushed up barking at her and was now licking her bare ankle. She looked around her. Patty's parents had money; they had property in B.C., and that was nothing to sneeze at. But Patty was living with her daughter upstairs from a chicken coop, about two hundred metres from their big house. Her place smelled. Like chickens, but also something else, something sadder. Julie wondered at her own luck. She went up the steps.

Patty hugged her. She didn't look distressed. In fact, she couldn't stop smiling. She opened a drawer and took out a small, square cardboard box. Angeline came bouncing into the room. She was dry-eyed. She greeted Julie with a hug around the waist before her gaze fell on the box.

"Is it for me? For me? For me?"

"No, it's not for you," Patty said crossly.

Julie watched her friend carefully. To her relief, Patty's voice softened as she continued. "Santa's bringing *your* presents—if you're good." She turned to Julie and said, "Max told Angeline that Santa exists, but most adults are just too stupid to realize it."

"*You* said it's the mothers and fathers who give the presents," Angeline said.

Patty ignored this remark and opened the box, pulling out what looked like a wooden clog. Julie looked mo
re closely: it was a man's head garishly painted with a bandana, eye patch and moustache. Patty handed it to Julie and laughed as it fell open in her lap, to reveal another smaller pirate's head, and then another, in the manner of a Russian doll.

"He won't even like it," Angeline said, pouting.

April. Mike came home from work, went straight to the TV and turned on the sports channel. Julie said, "Hello." He turned around quickly and said, "Oh, hi," as if he was surprised, had forgotten she lived there.

"I'm going out," she said as she put on her jacket. She told him that she was going to help Patty's friend with his college application. "Paul has that sleepover birthday party," she reminded him, "but he's never done this before, so maybe they'll call."

"Got it," Mike said, eyes on the screen.

Fifteen minutes late, Max rushed into the café. Black leather motor-cycle outfit clinging like a catsuit. He was coughing, smiling, gasping for breath.

"You're late," Julie said, instead of, "Are you all right?" At first, she regretted her rudeness, but then realized he hadn't noticed. He smiled and held up his right index finger.

He told her he would be right back and put his helmet on the table. He went out again before she could say anything. The helmet was big, black and shiny. It took up most of the table and, because it was sitting across from Julie, it seemed very incongruous, like a bowling ball next to a cup of tea. Julie was wearing a long skirt, sandals, and expertly coiffed hair; she'd gone to the hairdresser's that day.

Nearly twenty minutes late now. For his free lesson. A cloud of paranoia floated across Julie's mind. What had Patty said? That she was so bored with her life that she didn't mind correcting some foreigner's essay, for free? Suddenly, she missed her husband, who was responsible, never late and had acceptable manners. She remembered that he had a cold that morning, and she hadn't asked him how he was feeling before she left for the café.

She finally got up, walked to the front door and looked out. There Max was, sitting on the terrace, just a few feet away, smoking a cigarette, as if he had completely forgotten their appointment. She wondered if he thought he was good-looking. Maybe that was what this was all about.

Finally, he stubbed out his cigarette. Julie walked back to the table, took a paperback novel out of her bag, and pretended to be reading. She felt guilty and exhilarated. When he sat down, they smiled at each other. He took out two folded sheets of paper and handed them to her.

It was a letter about why he was applying to study at film school. The first page began beautifully.

"Sehr schön," Julie said.

Max repeated the words and smiled, nodding. She scrambled around in her memory for more German words, but couldn't find any at all.

The second page of the letter suddenly shifted into a mess of grammatical and spelling errors and run-on sentences.

"This isn't so good," she said apologetically, and noticed that he looked very disappointed. "Nope, nicht so gut." She felt very strange; everything felt strange. She wondered if she were speaking gibberish. She decided not to ask the obvious: was the first page heavily edited by a friend, or simply copied from a book? How could Max think she would fail to notice?

He leaned over and handed her another piece of folded paper. She opened it—it was blank—and heard a click. She looked up to see he was holding a camera.

"Don't like having your picture taken, do you? Oh, wonderful, here comes my sandwich."

He devoured his food in the space of a few seconds.

Then he looked at her with glinting wolfish eyes as if she were next.

"That must have been good," she said. "What kind of sandwich was that?"

"Meat," he said, and licked his lips.

Julie was appalled. She made an excuse to go home.

"Zo, I will make the corrections you ask for. Then we could meet again, if you have the time?"

They made an appointment to meet in two days. Two days, Julie thought, would give her time to calm down. Then she wondered why exactly she needed to calm down.

She decided that exercise might help her with whatever this was. Mike was already a member of a gym near his workplace. She hired a babysitter one evening and joined Mike in the weight room. She got on an exercise bike and looked across and watched her husband sitting on a leg-lift machine, forcing his poor, battered knees to perform. Their eyes met and he smiled a little. A man working out between her exercise bike and where Mike was sitting seemed to think the smile was for him, and he went over and talked to Mike. She smiled as she watched her husband gamely flirt back.

Afterwards, though, the thaw in their relationship disappeared.

In the car heading home, Julie made a crack about how long he had taken to get changed.

"What were you doing in that shower? What kind of man takes twice as long as his wife?"

He just glared at her. He clearly took it as a jibe, and not the light joke it had been intended to be. *Oh no*, thought Julie. *Our marriage is like one long culture shock.*

She met Max again at the same café. Outside the big window, rain fell like ink, blackening the day. Max was shivering. He had got soaked on his motorbike and his leather outfit was even glossier than usual. He sipped his hot coffee, holding the cup with shaking red hands, as Julie read over his work.

"Better?"

"Yes," Julie said. "But what is this word?"

They huddled together over the page. He smelled of tobacco and cold. She pointed to the letters "uge." The sentence said, "For many years I have felled the uge to be behind the camera, as opposed to somewhere of in a workshop constructing props for the directerr."

"Uhge," Max said. "I felt zuh uhge."

Julie smiled at him and corrected his spelling. His smile was so big it just barely fit his face. She tried to recall the last time Mike had smiled at her like that.

"Cold?" she asked.

"Ya, zis is some ugly weather," he said, with an exaggerated shudder. He made a funny little whirring noise, a foreign sort of noise.

Julie asked him if he had gone to the library to pick up the practice university entrance tests he had mentioned.

"Ach no. I will, though."

So they would see each other another time. Julie felt something leap happily in her chest.

"Well, I don't want to waste any more of your time," he said, taking both of their coffee bills and standing up.

So soon? Julie thought. She kept smiling. Everybody, she told herself, looked better with a smile.

He sneezed as he picked up his helmet and shook the water off his gloves.

"Can I ask you another favour?" he asked.

She nodded. He showed her a card from an art gallery on Venables Street. He wanted to know if she would drive him there. She agreed.

In the car, he asked her if she wanted to go to the gallery.

"Inside, I mean," he said.

"I don't know…"

"It is of the German Dada."

"I don't know much about art," Julie said.

"Me neither. But I know a little. I will show you. It is my turn."

As soon as they were enclosed together in the car, Julie felt nervous and embarrassed. The car seemed to fill with Max's wet-leather cigarette smell; the space they occupied together seemed too small, too intimate. Out of the corner of her eye, she noticed that his hands were still trembling despite the warmth of the car, and that he would not look in her direction at all.

The rain stopped as Julie parked. Light appeared in the sky. They walked past functional, ordinary, graceless city structures: mega-pharmacy, hardware store, laundromat, drycleaners. And, perhaps because of this ugly backdrop, something happened. Julie, catching her reflection in a window, was suddenly able to find beauty in herself. She saw a softness in her features that she liked. She allowed herself to notice Max too, how his hair was badly cut and attractively dishevelled, how the lines on his face seemed thoughtful. He had been looking at his boots, hands in pockets of shiny black pants, but now he turned, looked at her and finally smiled at her again in his generous way. It was as if a lighted mirror had been placed before her. She saw how the mist was making her hair curl, wavy strands pulling free of ties and barrettes, how slender her arms were, and how absurdly bare on this cold grey morning. She shivered and hugged herself. He put his arm around her and they entered the gallery. She felt a shock shoot through her arm and wondered if he could feel it. She also wondered if they looked like a couple.

Inside, Max and the woman behind the counter kissed hello and exchanged a few words in German. Julie asked him a moment later how they knew each other, but he shook his head and shrugged.

The gallery was cream-coloured, with spotless carpets that sloped into different rooms. The walls were glass; the pictures exhibited on long, rectangular panels. Each picture was a collage of photographs of European politicians, of whom Julie could recognize only three—and speech bubbles. Max chuckled to himself as he wandered around the room.

Julie felt stupid. Max walked ahead of her for a moment, and then turned and looked into her eyes. She remembered how he had greeted the unknown German woman, and turned away.

But then he touched her arm, said, "Come," in a quiet voice, and with gentle patience, told her everything he knew about the "German Dada," which turned out to be a lot.

After failing yet another college-entry English test, Max called Julie and asked for more help. They met a few times, and he was suitably serious. But always late.

One day, toward the end of their meeting, she looked around at the series of canvasses on the wall of the café. They depicted scenes from a particularly bloody nightmare. Ghoulish, stricken faces, loads of red paint. She asked Max what he thought of them.

"Not much," he answered, shrugging, "but maybe I just can't relate to them somehow."

"I have a present for you," Julie said.

Max greeted this news the way a child would. His face betrayed no surprise, only a kind of entitlement, but his grin was nevertheless wide and excited.

41

"Well," he said, pulling at her sleeve from across the table, "what is it? What is it?"

Julie had done an outrageous thing. She had bought him a watch. An artsy sort of watch—turquoise strap, Matisse-like cut-out figure, running around the face. She had spent almost a hundred dollars on someone she barely knew. The fact was not lost on Max, she realized. A fleeting look. Then, back to his breezy, charming manner.

"Thank you. How sweet of you. Oh wonderful, here comes my sandwich."

Before they parted, Max invited Julie to a party the following Friday night. Julie wondered about this all the way home, and then all week. She wondered if Mike would care, and whether or not she wanted him to.

When she got home, before she could take her coat off, Paul ran to her, shouting excitedly.

"Somebody called three times, Mummy," Paul told her, showing her three fingers.

The teenage babysitter apologized for letting him answer the phone.

Julie reassured her. "Nobody ever calls, hence the excitement," she explained.

"She said she wanted to speak to Daddy," Paul added.

Julie put her purse on a chair and then leaned against it for a moment.

"Who?" she asked.

"Don't remember," Paul said, suddenly more interested in a bag of licorice the babysitter had just opened. "She had a funny name. A name like a sneeze."

On Friday night Patty called to tell Julie she was going to the party.

"And you wanted to know if we would babysit?" Julie asked.

"Hey, it's okay. My parents said they would if you couldn't."

She went on to ask her if she wanted to come along.

"Oh, you figured you'd invite me at the last minute," Julie said. Something red was rising in her. She told her that she was going too, that someone else had invited her, and that Mike had agreed to watch Paul.

"What?" Patty laughed, incredulous. "Who invited you?"

Julie realized she had painted herself into a corner. She needed to control herself. Patty's laughter was triggering more of this surprising anger.

"I can't talk about it right now," she muttered into the phone. She felt like a character in a film, one with secrets. "I'll see you later."

Mike frowned but said nothing. Julie noticed that he had mashed potatoes in his hair. Paul was screaming, singsong, "Mummy, Mummy, Mummy," and Julie wondered vaguely how long he had been calling her. The sinks and counters were so full of dirty dishes and pots that they had started a new pile on the floor.

I have to get out of here, Julie thought. *If I don't, I'm going to turn into one of those mothers in the newspapers who drive their kids into a lake.*

The stereo was blaring. Julie wondered if Max could hear his doorbell. The door opened; Max grinned, then shook his sleeve and lifted his arm to show her his wrist. The watch.

"Right on time," he said.

Julie blushed, and was grateful that the apartment was barely lit. The music was even louder now that she was inside. It was dark, thrusting and male, but also pretty, melodic and bittersweet.

"Sorry," Max said unexpectedly, and turned down the volume. Somehow the effect continued to emanate from Max's eyes, which were at once ice-cold and wolfish, long-lashed and sensitive.

Julie told him she liked the music and asked if he would make her a tape.

"Yes, of course. I am delighted. Whiskey?"

"I'm driving," Julie reminded him.

"Ya, okay. You drive, I drink." He took a sip of his drink, made a face. "That's enough."

"Patty's going to this party, isn't she?" Julie said.

"Is she?" Max said. He thought for a moment. "Ah, but I have just thought of another party we can go to!"

Who would have thought, after getting married and having a kid, Julie would be driving down city streets late on a Saturday night, a foreign stranger next to her with his smell of cigarettes, leather and whiskey. Where were they going? Max gestured, right here, straight ahead, left, right.

As they got out of the car, Max let out a yelp and began to run. At the entrance of a nondescript warehouse, a tall, bland-featured man wearing glasses and a trenchcoat stood. Max whooped, jumped into the man's arms, and turned to Julie to beckon her forward.

"Come, Julie. Meet my very good friend Brian."

Inside, a tiny man wearing a fedora recited poetry on stage, backed by a jazz quartet. Brian picked up one of Julie's hands and looked into her eyes.

"Brian's a great photographer," Max said. "He likes very much to look at people."

Brian ignored him and examined Julie's hand.

"Do you play the piano, Julie?" he asked.

"Yes, a little," Julie said, giggling. She felt like an impostor. She wasn't a student, an artist or a musician. She was a married woman with a kid. She wasn't even unemployed.

"But you don't have one, do you?" Brian said.

"A piano? No. Can you tell that from looking at my hands too?"

He ignored the question, and instead announced that he was going to Russia.

"Have a nice time," Julie said. She turned to watch the poet and the band.

"I could leave my piano at your house, if you'd like," he said. "Then you could play."

"What's he saying to you, that one?" Max asked, as if Brian weren't there.

Brian explained about the piano.

"Would you like to have a piano?" Max asked her now.

"I'd love to," Julie said, as if accepting an invitation to a ball. Then she realized how much she actually would. She thought of Mike at home, watching TV, how lonely it was when Paul went to bed, how long it had been since she had played, how beautiful a room seemed when filled with the romantic, rippling peals of a piano.

To her surprise, both Brian and Max were watching her face, not speaking.

"I don't have a truck or anything," she said. "And we'd need a lot of people. I don't even know anybody."

Max was nodding thoughtfully. The poet and band had left the stage. The three of them sat together, not talking. She glanced at Max's face, and remembered, with a pang, falling in love with Mike.

She drove Max home about three hours past her normal bedtime. She had had one drink all evening, but it was so late that fatigue and inebriation were indistinguishable; she felt transported, if only into another time zone. It had been so long since she'd driven along roads so still, through a night so black. Devoid of traffic, the streets flew by swiftly, and, as if by magic, the car arrived at Max's street.

Max asked her if she had enjoyed the poetry. There had been a few different people on stage, but she could no longer remember any of them.

"Yes, did you?"

"No," he said, yawning. "I wasn't really listening."

"Are you really going to bring me a piano?" she asked, as he leaned over to give her a polite peck on the cheek.

He paused. "Ya, that should be a fun thing."

"And are you going to want piano lessons too?" she blurted out.

He laughed. "Ya, ya, I saw that movie too."

She reached out, touched one of his cheeks and gave him a small kiss on the lips.

He didn't react as if he had been bitten. He wanted more. She said, "Sorry." He took the hint and got out of the car.

A September day. Bright, but chilly, like a morning. Mike took the day off work to go to the dentist's and to an eye specialist. Julie dropped him off at the dentist's, ran some errands and then picked him up from the eye doctor's. They had twenty-five minutes to kill before it was time to get Paul, so Julie suggested to Mike, as if to a stranger, to have a cup of coffee somewhere together.

They sat across from each other in silence. Julie played a little game with herself: *I won't speak unless Mike actually says something to me.* But there was no sound from Mike, aside from the cold metal ring of his spoon hitting the side of his mug. They sat like that until it was almost time to go. Then, suddenly, Julie couldn't take it anymore.

"Why are we still together?" she blurted out.

"Hmmmm?" Mike met her eyes, and looked more amused than surprised.

She felt lost, felt like she could float away. She hoped he would give her a definitive answer that would nail her to the ground.

And he did.

"Because of our son." His gaze was a cool warning.

Julie thought of all the other things he could have said: We love each other. We make love. Because despite the cold silence they lived in, they still sought out each other's heat in the night, unthinking, unconscious, like two animals of a lower species. Underwater creatures.

"So what if one of us meets someone else?" she asked, fighting back tears.

"We'll cross that bridge when we come to it."

Julie thought of an excuse to call Max. He liked art galleries. She would invite him to visit the VAG.

He agreed. They met downtown. He was wearing his leather gear, a t-shirt that said, "Shoot clean, fuck safe," two silk scarves around his neck, and, around his waist, a seat belt that seemed to have come from an airplane. She heard Patty's voice in her head: "He is *so cool.*"

The display puzzled her at first. A shelf of glass bottles filled with beads, a woven rug, thatched walls. Then, on a small wicker table, an open copy of *National Geographic* with what seemed to be a photograph of that scene. They walked on, visiting more scenes from life in the Third World.

"They're good, aren't they?" Julie said. She wasn't sure what she was looking at.

"Mmmm," said Max. "It's pretty much what *I* do."

"Oh, that's right. You're a set builder."

"Ya, they give me a picture, like this, and I just copy it."

"That's amazing. How do you know what kind of materials to use? How do you know where to begin?"

"The cheapest. The cheapest materials, the cheapest way. As long as it looks good, they're happy. But it's all fake, of course. Just blow on it,"—he paused and blew—"and it all falls down."

"And do you get paid well for all this cheap work?"

"Ya, actually, I get paid quite a lot."

Later, as they left the gallery, Max said in his light, singsong voice, "Dinnertime. Your husband waits for you now."

Julie thought about what to say to this. Finally, she said, "Yes."

They had come to the gallery separately, Julie in her beige hatchback, Max on his gleaming black motorcycle. He walked toward his bike, sat down and revved up the engine.

That's it. No kiss. Julie felt both relief and disappointment. *I didn't really have the stomach for this. I'll just drive home now, back to my life.*

Max said something that was lost in the motorbike's roar. Julie pointed to her ears, shook her head and shrugged.

"Sorry," he said, as the bike went into idle, "Fucking noisy bugger, this one."

"It's okay," Julie said quickly. "I kind of like the noise."

Max raised his eyebrows, put his head to one side in an exaggerated, quizzical way. Like someone who was not really interested, only humouring her. On his bike, ready to go. But Julie couldn't help it; the words came gushing out.

"It's very quiet at home. We live in this sort of rural suburb. It is very isolating. I live in a house that is just so... so cold. My husband never talks to me. Ever."

Max was looking at her intently as she spoke. His gaze warmed her for a moment; then, the theatrical eyebrow thing returned and, suddenly angry with both of them, she turned and walked towards her car.

As she started her engine, she heard him calling her. She rolled down her window.

"What?"

"I was saying... I said... it sounds like you could really use a piano."

*

One evening Patty called Julie and invited her over to watch a little film.

"Max made it," she said. "We were wondering if you would be interested in translating it and dubbing it in French. Do you think you could pretend to be a little girl?"

Julie was too surprised to speak.

"He is applying to film school all over Canada, you know," said Patty.

She didn't know. She wondered why he hadn't asked her himself. What was this "we"?

"It's not the sort of thing he usually makes," Patty was saying, "you know, experimental stuff featuring fire, people on drugs, avant-garde music… "

Instead, the subject of the film was little Angeline, who talked to the camera about herself.

"I am only in kindergarten because I was sick last year so I missed a lot of school, and I can only count to thirteen and you have to be able to count to twenty. I live with my mother in the chickenhouse, but upstairs. My grandparents live in the other house, just across the yard. My father lives in Montreal, and he said he was coming to visit us, but then when we got to the airport, he wasn't even there. We have a little dog, and once she ate a pile of shit, so now we call her Sheila the shit-hound."

Patty watched the movie. Julie watched it too, but glanced often at her friend's face.

"I wish I didn't have hair like this," Angeline was saying, pulling on her dense curls. "I wish my hair was yellow and straight and pretty like my cousin's."

"He loves her," Patty said wistfully.

"Yeah," Julie agreed.

Later that week, Mike and Julie had guests to supper: two young women, Rikako and Yuki, and a young man named Hiro who seemed to be their common boyfriend, or some kind of pet. They were students from the university where Julie worked. They offered to come over and cook Julie and Mike supper at their house. Julie hesitated at first, but gradually understood that if she didn't accept she might be committing a grave social error. She envied them this, their rules, the security of always knowing what to do. She told them, though, that such an offer was unheard of in Canada.

"You can do it, but you know, if you go to much trouble you will make us, your hosts, feel bad." She enjoyed their momentary uncertainty as they digested this information.

"In this case," said Yuki, who had a strikingly angular haircut, "we will bring only packaged foods."

Mike picked them up after work, and they all enjoyed a feast of Ramen noodles. Paul was thrilled and willingly sat in laps and exchanged exotic clapping games with the guests. After a while, Rikako, who was tall and wore her hair in ribboned braids, announced that they had a gift.

"We did not want to embarrass you," said Yuki. "So we spent no money."

Giggling, both girls nudged Hiro.

"Ah," Julie said in a bold voice, "so Hiro is my present."

Mike gave her a look.

"This is my job," Julie muttered to Mike.

She thanked the girls for the present. "I never thought you would part with him."

"No, you see, they want me to sing," explained Hiro. "But I told them that I only sing with music."

"Daddy plays the clarinet," offered Paul. Mike said nothing. There was an awkward pause.

"Well, Mummy says he does," Paul added.

"He leaves it at work," Julie said without an explanation, since, as far as she was concerned, there was none. "I am sorry, Hiro. You will have to do it a cappella."

She was asking him if he knew what that meant when Rikako shook her head vigorously, waving her finger. She was looking out the window and had evidently seen something she had no words for.

The five of them—everyone but Mike—crowded before the wide living room window and watched as something resembling a Trojan horse made its halting way across their muddy front yard. It was raining; it was hard to see, but Paul and Rikako agreed that there were at least eight pairs of legs involved in this scene. And some kind of structure, and a black… tarp? Then someone ran ahead, and with a pang of guilt, Julie realized it was Patty. She watched as her friend set a dolly on the ground.

"Mummy," Paul cried. "It's a piano! And more friends! Mummy, we can have a real party now!"

As Mike shot Julie an angry look, Max appeared in the doorway, his eyes registering Mike's expression. He nodded at the group and said nothing. He was out of breath. Julie introduced everyone to him.

"Ah, you are Julie's students. I am charmed to meet you."

Rikako explained that they were students, but not Julie's. "But Julie is helpful to us, like a good teacher."

"And you? You are a friend? This piano is a surprise, no?" asked Yuki.

"No, I am just a student," Max replied. "I just wanted to thank Julie for being something like a good teacher."

The Japanese girls exchanged a disconcerted look. Max spotted Paul, who was staring at him with his wide, dark eyes, and bent forward to give him a poke in the stomach.

A chorus of youngish voices called Max's name. A group of men and women, most of them in leather jackets, their hair soaking wet and sticking to their faces, were leaning on the piano, which was halfway up the front stairs.

"I wanna help," Paul cried in his flutey voice.

"Yes, of course," Max answered. "Can you say, 'Heave ho, heave ho'?"

Several heave ho's later the piano emerged through the doorway, followed by Max's friends.

Afterwards, they all sat on the floor and listened to a man called Skunk play the piano. Patty told Julie that she had been wondering why Max wouldn't come out dancing with her that night. "He said he got roped into delivering this piano."

"He used those words, did he?" Julie asked. Strange how, when she should have been feeling incredibly grateful, honoured, loved, even, everything seemed complicated and stressful. Maybe because Mike was standing at the entrance to the living room by himself, glaring at everyone.

Max, sitting across the room with his chin in his palm, looked up at her then, his eyes gleaming like a cat's.

Max got accepted at film school at S.F.U. To pay for his courses, he moved to a cheaper neighbourhood, began to do construction jobs, and put his little films on hold. When Julie called him with a question about the film she was dubbing, he asked her to meet him at an unfinished house he was working on, and bring the tape with her. He told her he would be alone.

"You're working on a house alone?"

"Ya, I don't work too good with other people."

When she arrived at the address in North Vancouver, she was startled to see that there were no walls yet. Exposed wooden struts, nails sticking out of boards. She heard the sharp screech of a chainsaw. She peeked around a corner and saw a cloud of smoke-filled dust and Max in a toolbelt, leather pants, woodchips in his hair. A cigarette was dangling from his mouth, and his face was tight with concentration as he bent close to a table to cut a piece of wood. When he looked up and noticed her, he let the cigarette and wood fall to the floor, and beamed.

He held his arms out to her. His sleeves were rolled up to reveal his muscles, strange on such a slight body, and his skin, a striking coppery brown. They hugged, and he led her around the naked broken house, up a narrow half-built staircase, to the roof. The sky was overcast. There was a dreary murmur of traffic below. He showed her where he had tripped a few days before, lurched backwards, flown three stories down, and then landed miraculously on his feet.

"My cat!" she heard herself say, surprising both of them. She put her hand up under his shirt and stroked his back. He purred. She looked at him wonderingly, dimly, almost recognizing something.

"Well, I'd better get back to work," he said, stretching, yawning, and winking. He gave her a gentle push toward the hole in the roof.

There were two steps missing. She wondered what would happen if she fell through. How would she land?

Downstairs again she started to say she had to go too, a million things to do before she had to go pick up Paul, but then suddenly he was grabbing her and walking her over to one of the worktables. There were more nails, tools, sawdust, splintery projects everywhere, but he didn't swipe anything aside as he pushed her down on a table and leaned over her, opening her mouth with his, washing it again and again with heavy strokes of his tongue. She was not comfortable; she could feel the shape of a drill under the curve of her back and wondered if it was plugged in—but she lay back with a sigh and let her mouth answer his. Then, feeling more dizzy than aroused, she fell into a dream.

She became conscious of her surroundings again when he leaned back and she heard him reach into his back pocket and rip open a condom. She soon felt stabs of pure pleasure, but it ended quickly and she fell back into a dream as he rested in her arms.

She opened her eyes to see a dusty sunbeam falling on them. The grey had gone. What time was it? She glanced at the chaos around her, remembering, thinking of the errands awaiting her, and then, with alarm, of Paul, who would be looking out the window, brown eyes grave, understanding only that she wasn't there.

A few days later, Paul was excited: a rare bus journey. He stared at everything and everybody with round brown eyes. Julie held him by a belt loop as he kneeled and gazed out the window. They sailed across their rural enclave, crossed the bridge into town, quickly passed synagogues, temples, a shopping mall and a church, residential streets of hodgepodge houses, each structure ill-fitting in its own way. Paul, suddenly overwhelmed and exhausted, collapsed and slept in Julie's lap.

Then, as they approached the Downtown Eastside, where Max had recently moved, the bus began to fill with street people. Sassy, gum-chewing prostitutes; jittery, pencil-thin drug addicts; a chocolate-brown transvestite in a red wig—Paul woke up, his jaw comically open, as he began to sing—and people so poor and bedraggled they looked like characters from a nativity scene.

They arrived at Max's street, a row of abandoned warehouses inhabited by artists. Julie instructed Paul to get up and ring the bell and as he did an old woman in a blanket dropped into his seat and pressed a coin into his hand.

"Wow! A loonie!" Paul exclaimed as they prepared to jump off the bus. "What did she give me that for?"

"I guess because you gave her your seat."

"But we were getting off anyway," Paul said, frowning at his treasure. Then he looked up at the people and the sidewalk around him. A woman with long, stringy grey hair shouted, "Hey!" at them. A little person was relieving himself in what Julie suddenly realized was Max's doorway. Someone had written "'Jesus lives here" on the boarded-up window. When the little man had finished, Julie said, "Excuse me," and he let them pass.

"It smells," Paul said.

They knocked on the door and waited for what seemed like minutes. Julie wondered if Max had forgotten about their visit. *That would be like him.* But the door swung open and there he was, crying, "Welcome, my sweeties," in his wonderfully exotic way. He cupped each of their faces in his hands and planted a noisy kiss on their lips, like an elderly foreign aunt. He was wearing an orange shirt covered with cartoon cowboys and Indians. It was long, almost reaching his knees.

Suddenly he held up a finger, swung around, then back, and began to cough violently, managing to utter, "Something in my throat," between loud, plaintive barks. Paul looked alarmed. Finally, Max made a spitting noise, and *seemed* to spit on the floor, ending the coughing fit. A theatrical pause, and then he bent down very low and picked up four miniature farm animals, a tiny plastic revolver, a toy car, two marbles, a die.

"I knew there was something in my throat," he told them. "Here, you'd better take them." He stuffed Paul's little palms.

Take us away, Julie thought. *Put on a cowboy hat. Get on a white horse, and come to our house at midnight. We'll be waiting.*

But when Max finally looked at her and returned her smile, his was grave and apologetic. *This is all I've got*, is what it said.

On a whim, Julie decided to invite Max to Paul's birthday party. The two were lovers now; they were each other's habit. Paul had invited five small friends. The children drew pictures on the paper tablecloth as they waited for Julie to serve them juice and cake. Mike had to go to his studio but was due to return in a few hours. Julie wondered if Max would show, and if so, when. He could be counted on to be late. She wondered whether there would be awkwardness if he arrived at the same time as Mike. She was standing on a chair, wearing a white apron, trying to reach a bottle of juice in the cupboard over the fridge. The children were calling out their orders, not realizing they would all have to settle for the same generic fruit blend. Julie had a headache. The phone rang, startling her. The bottle flew out of her hands, hitting two of the seated children, before shattering on the table. Blood-coloured liquid washed over the table.

Some of the children were shrieking, but Paul was oblivious. He ran to answer the phone, shouting, "My birthday, for me."

"Hello? Oh, hi Max."

Julie gathered up the tablecloth and mopped up the mess. A sliver of glass stung her right palm. The children wanted to know when they could have their apple, orange and grape juice. There was also a request for Orange Crush.

When Paul had hung up, Julie asked what Max had wanted, and whether he was coming.

"He said, *Are you having fun?*"

"And?"

"And I said yes."

55

"And?"

"He wanted to know my favourite colour rope."

"Rope?"

"Yes, I think so."

An hour later, the children were running around upstairs and Julie was still cleaning up in the kitchen when there was a knock on the door. It was Max, in a motorbike helmet and his leather suit. In his hands, a metal toolbox, a small plank of wood, and a few feet of orange rope.

"Where are the kids?" he asked, as they kissed. She pointed upstairs, towards the noise of complete chaos.

"I like it," he said thoughtfully.

"And what's this?" Julie asked, indicating the pile of rope.

"A present for Paul. But it's for everybody, really."

"Everybody?"

"Anyway, get out of here, woman," he said, pulling at her apron and then pushing her away. "To the kitchen now. I have work to do."

Twenty minutes later, Mike was the first to see Max's present. Julie stood in the doorway of the kitchen to see Mike standing in the entrance, looking enraged. In the hallway between the living room and the kitchen, Max had installed a swing. Both men looked at Julie.

"Want to try it out?" Max asked her.

"It won't bear her weight," Mike said.

"Oh, I don't know," Julie said, putting on a falsely polite voice, pretending that she had to be careful with Max's feelings, that he was merely a foreign stranger she had to be gentle with. She was acutely aware that the two men had not said hello to each other.

"Oh well," Max said. "It was just for a little fun. Maybe let it stay for as long as it does."

He asked if Angeline was there. Julie shook her head. She hadn't invited her, afraid she wouldn't be able to look her mother in the eye.

"Oh," said Max. "I could have taken her home on the motor-bike."

Mike rolled his eyes, brushed by Julie, and opened the fridge.

Max said he had to leave. He pointed upstairs, where a collective giggle, a ball, and some sort of wheeled toy were rolling around noisily. "You give your boy a big smooch for me."

Julie walked him outside, wondering if he would dare kiss her in front of her house. His eyes were soft and lost in thought. He told her he was disappointed not to see Angeline.

"You know, I often used to wish I was attracted to Patty, since I get along so well with her. I think that little girl could really use another adult in her life."

Julie watched him, surprised.

"At first, she never trusted me," he told her. "Patty had these feelings for me, and she didn't like that. And you know, this father of hers always saying he's gonna show up, and he never does."

Julie found it strange to hear Max describe himself as more depend-able than someone else. She had never met someone who was more consistently late. She had a feeling nobody had ever told him off. She felt like screaming at him sometimes, but knew it wasn't appropriate, given their sort of relationship. Their *affair*. Patty wouldn't scream at him either, she realized, being hopelessly in love.

Instead, she remembered dully, she screamed at her daughter.

The party guests were picked up by their parents. Supper, dishes, bath, bedtime stories. Mike was lying in front of the TV lifting weights. Julie was about to go upstairs to bed but stopped. Something itched. She peeled down her underwear and showed the bumps to Mike. He just stared at her. She shrugged and went upstairs.

But later the weight of his body awakened her. His tongue was in her mouth, his hands on her hips—and suddenly, he turned away. She turned over and watched him, far on the other side of the bed now, and on his back, staring up at the ceiling.

He said nothing for a long time, but then he began a long ramble, something about wanting to figure out what wasn't working, cycling somewhere to buy her flowers, something he realized he had never, in all these years, done, finding none, being unable to get the image of her pulling down her underwear out of his head, exercising furiously in his strange, tormented state.

"I was about to rape you just now," he explained with such self-loathing that she let herself melt and took him in her arms.

"You're no rapist, Mike. You don't have it in you," Julie cooed, holding him.

After they made love she saw an owl staring at them from the window, and when she made Mike look, it flew away. Such a strange night. Something was starting to break down in her, her depression, and also some kind of icy resolve.

Why, oh why, did she lend him her car? Julie had told Max that her meeting would finish at two, but it was already past three o'clock. Everyone else had left. The couple who hosted the meeting, one of her colleagues and her husband, had very clean beige carpets. They smiled at her as they passed by where she waited, in the hallway.

She tried calling Max's pager, but it wasn't on.

It was probably her fault. If she hadn't drunk so much coffee, she wouldn't be this anxious. But he had Paul with him. She imagined the car sliding out of control, her little boy's head hitting the windshield. He drove so fast. She'd already paid three speeding tickets for him, completing the task before Mike asked any questions.

Suddenly there was a clamour outside. Max was grinning. Paul looked tired, but all right. James, the colleague's husband, opened the door as they came up the steps. Julie watched the expression in his eyes as he smiled politely, taking in Max's leather outfit, his unshaven face.

"Where were you?" she demanded.

Max shot her a quick look.

"The kid was hungry," he said. "So we went out for pancakes."

Paul didn't smile. Paul hated pancakes.

It was past ten o'clock. Julie had been at a work party and should have been on her way home. Instead, she found herself knocking on Max's door. One knock. She was tired; that was all she was willing to give.

She heard him jump down from his loft. Here he was, here was his kiss, and here was a surprise: a sinking feeling of disappointment so strong and clear that she groaned out loud.

Max didn't notice. "I'm so glad you got my message," he said, clasping her hands and pulling her to him. She felt energy draining away from her body and closed her eyes.

"You need food," Max announced, and led her to a chair. On the table, Max's peanut-chicken-cream-cheese concoction, an original recipe of his, the only thing, she noticed, he ever made.

Something smelled bad.

"This would taste better," she said between bites, "if you added a vegetable or two."

Something smelled like shit.

"I can't finish this," she said.

"No problem," Max said, jumping up and taking her plate away. "Now you can help me with my homework."

He said this as if he believed this was some kind of treat for her. He took her hand and pulled her up from the chair. They were just about to climb the ladder to the loft when she noticed a trail of brown smudges approaching the first step, and, on the first step itself, a small but unmistakable pile of excrement.

"Max, what is this?" Julie demanded.

He looked down and scowled. "I know, I know. I'm going to kill that dog."

"What dog?"

"That one that lives next door. I left my door open this morning, and the beast came in and decided, 'This is the place.'" Max imitated a dog squatting and defecating.

"This morning?"

"Yes, I do get up in the morning sometimes, you know."

"And you haven't cleared it up yet?"

"I will, don't worry. But now, come help me with my homework! You're getting tired and cranky. Soon it will be too late for you to help me."

Max patted her bum and gave her a push up the steps. He put her in a swivel chair in front of his computer and leaned over her, manoeuvring the mouse. A skull and crossbones, his personal insignia, appeared on the screen. He clicked onto a blank page. His homework, he explained, was an essay about a film presented in class a month earlier.

"You haven't started this?" Julie shouted, exasperated.

"Easy, Julie," Max whispered, breathing into her ear. "I have a couple of ideas."

It took her forty-five minutes to rebel. Having written a page and a half about a film she had never seen, she lifted his arms from around her neck, pushed the chair back with her feet and announced she was too tired to continue.

"You said you'd help me."

But it was the same petulant whine she had learned to ignore in her son, so she thanked him for the cream-cheese surprise, headed down the stairs, carefully stepped over the dog poo and went out the door.

The air, even here on Skid Row, was fresh and almost fragrant. She got into her car and drove home, feeling all the way like a person driving a car in a TV commercial: free. A half-hour later she was at home between clean sheets, next to her sleeping husband, who smelled of soap.

Four evenings in a row since she said goodbye there were flowers on her windshield when she returned to her car after work. The paper around the stems disintegrating, leaving cottony dust on the glass. She glanced at the flowers briefly before tossing them on the floor of the passenger seat. *Narcissus.*

What did he imagine Mike would think, Julie wondered, if she brought these inside the house and put them in a vase?

Max's voice on the phone. "Are you sitting down?"

"Yes. Why?" she said coldly.

His last call, he'd breathed noisily, obviously cold, and told her he was calling from a tunnel in White Rock. He was on his motorcycle and had run out of gas. She rescued him then but warned him it was the last time. Now what?

"Julie, Patty is HIV-positive."

She felt torn. But she really did not want to talk to Max, and anyway, she hadn't seen Patty for a long time.

"So, well, you know, I slept with Patty a few times. You know that, right?"

"No," Julie said, shocked. She suddenly realized she should have known.

"I can't remember if I used a condom."

"You always did with me," said Julie. *Except once.*

"I don't know. It's something we did when we were both very drunk."

"Who gave it to her?" Julie asked, after a pause.

"She doesn't know."

She doesn't know. The words sank in slowly. The whole conversation struck her as absurd. Patty was not the promiscuous type. She was more interested in food and art. She got a little fatter every year. Clearly this should have happened to someone else.

Finally it hit her, what he was trying to say.

The fear. It was squeezing the breath from her. She looked outside and saw that she would have to pretend again. An audience awaited.

Julie's parents were visiting from Montreal. They sat on the front lawn in white plastic chairs. At the edge of the lawn was a dike. At first, she had thought it was a natural pond, as it was full of ducks and fish, but it was just an artificial dike, dug out to irrigate the cranberry fields, and it was also full of farm chemicals. Two willows stood waist-high in the murky water, branches and leaves swooping down, skimming the surface. The landlord's black Lab, Jesse, fetched a ball Paul kept throwing in the water. Over and over, the same scene: the dog trotted to the edge of the lawn, stumbled down the bank and fell into the water with a great splash. Paul screamed with laughter. Jesse was oblivious to all but the ball. Upon retrieving it, he ran back, panting and salivating but never relinquishing the object of his obsession, until, ignoring Paul, he dropped it at the grandfather's feet. Then, as if suddenly noticing that he was soaking wet, he shook himself with such force that he sprayed everyone at once.

Julie thought of sneaking away inside and taking a shower. She imagined crying alone under the spray. Almost surpassing her fear now was the desperate need to be alone.

Mike came outside wearing a white t-shirt. The shirt billowed around his body in the wind. He shielded his eyes from the sunlight as he glanced at his wife, then turned and watched Jesse's antics. He and Julie's parents shared a joke about the dog. Julie heard Mike say something that ended with "go to work now." So normal. He seemed very far away. She couldn't imagine telling him.

She drove Mike to work. They lived at the end of a country road, bordered on both sides by farms, cows grazing on one side, cranberry fields on the other. A bit of countryside hidden away at the edge of the city, incongruous, a surprise to drivers who sometimes lost their way while test-driving cars from the nearby auto mall. Julie knew that although they had never had a conversation about it, they had both chosen this place because they imagined the serenity of the cows, the beauty of the willows, and especially the quiet of the country road would offer them refuge, privacy and protection. That away from the stresses and temptations of the city, their relationship could heal. Julie stopped the car in front of the entrance to the studio.

Instead of getting out of the car, Mike surprised her by suggesting they sit in the car and enjoy the quiet for a few minutes.

Julie realized that he just meant a few minutes away from his job and her parents. She looked at his face and suddenly saw a strong resemblance to their son's. She was struck very hard with remorse. She had to tell him, she had to get tested and have him tested, and strangely, she felt a giant surge of lust for him now, over everything, over all the pain and remorse and fear.

Mike's eyes met hers. He raised his eyebrows, and waited. She hadn't been pretending very well at all. Her eyes had filled with tears. He stroked her arm, but his fingers felt very light, as if he were afraid to touch her. "Tell me," he said.

And so she began, her first words expelled with a gasp.

A short dream, like one of Max's little films, shot on overexposed 8-mm film. Max was in jail. Lots of white light, and, through silvery bars, there he was, a small silent figure in loose white cotton prison garb. Julie had come to visit. They stared at each other through the bars. To her surprise, the prison guard arrived with an enormous set of keys and let her into the cell.

After some time, a buzzer sounded. The visit was over.

But the guard didn't come back.

The terror inside her. Julie looked at the blue wall, tried to drown in the blue. The look in the grey-haired nurse's eyes as she read the small slip of paper, the look she tried to mask as she smiled and asked Julie to roll up her sleeve. Her sea-green eyes, her simple, clean, well-ironed blouse, a smell of hotel soap. A tiny pain in the spot which she so quickly wiped clean, the burning, dizzying smell of alcohol. Her cool, yet sympathetic expression. Julie imagined begging her to clean her all over, to prick her all over, to take her back to her immaculate, freshly-painted house, put her to bed in the guest bedroom with the pale yellow curtains and nothing to look at on the wall.

"When will I know the results?"

"Oh, in a week or two."

"One? Or two?"

But it was of no use. The doctor had already given her the same answer. "Call us in a week or two. Sometimes it's earlier. Sometimes it's six days." She would have liked to shake him. But she just listened and nodded as if this obedient behaviour would improve the chances of a negative result.

"Help me," she wanted to say to this woman now. "I want to be knocked unconscious for two weeks."

At home, Mike maintained his stony silence. She knew that inside, anger and fear were churning; she remembered reading a definition of hate which had mentioned fear as its primary component. Mike hated her so much he could not bear to look at her. Her parents, understanding nothing, yet acutely aware of the freezing atmosphere, moved about with uncharacteristic cautiousness, and she knew they blamed themselves for whatever was happening. She noticed that they had suddenly begun to look old. Her heart was shattering in a hundred different places.

Outside it had turned very hot; even the wind burned. Paul jumped through the sprinkler, shrieking, his uncomplicated happiness so close as to be almost tangible, yet beyond his parents' grasp.

Days passed. Days of Julie sneaking into her bedroom to perform the frantic morning dialing ritual. First, the call to the doctor's office. The call was taken by an answering service: the doctors were never in on time. The woman on the other end of the line was completely anonymous—"Doctors' Answering Service" was how she answered the phone—but Julie felt sure she knew her by now; they went through this every day.

"Not in yet?" she asked.

"No," the woman replied, with equal futility. "Try again in a few minutes."

Later, the "real" receptionist put her on hold, returned after an excruciating five minutes, and, showing no sign that she had any conception of the inadequacy of the response, nor that they had already had this conversation five or six times, announced, "They are not in yet. We don't know when they will be. We will call you sometime after they come in, but if you'd like to, you can call back." Her tone never varied and she never veered from her script.

Julie's parents left. She watched them walk into the airport together. They seemed to stumble like toddlers and hang on to each other for balance. She wondered when they had gotten so heartbreakingly old. But at least, she thought, they got to be old.

With her parents gone she relaxed a bit, let herself cry, swore at herself, plead for forgiveness. Paul didn't seem to notice that his mother no longer ate, nor that his father no longer spoke to her. When she broke down in the middle of supper, he actually giggled as he asked what was happening to her.

At night, she said to Mike, "The waiting is killing me, but your silence…"

He pulled the sheets over himself and turned away. She lay awake, imagining the two of them buried next to each other.

And then, one day, the temperature cooled and the sky filled with black clouds. Mike spoke to Julie for the first time in days: he curtly asked permission to take the car, rather than his bicycle, to work, as she had called in sick. The morning was so dark that he put on his headlights as he backed out of the driveway.

The phone rang. She felt the blood rush as she rose to her feet. She wondered if coursing along with the blood were rapidly multiplying HIV cells. Her legs hurt, her own fault, she told herself: if she had spent more time playing with her son than indulging herself in dangerous adventures outside the house, she would be more supple. When she reached the phone the ringing seemed to ring louder, more insistently, waking her from her guilty reverie. She allowed herself the small hope that the call would deliver the news she needed to hear.

"This is the Second Street Medical Clinic," the voice at the other end of the phone said. "Your results are in, but we can't give them to you on the phone. Dr. Sutherland would like to speak to you in person. Can you come in today?"

The cab smelled like coffee, leather and aftershave. It smelled like a perfect father. Lightning flashed by the windows. Then the sky roared and it started to rain. Julie felt lifted across the five or six kilometres. As the taxi pulled up beside the clinic, she was able to look through its glass walls and see Dr. Sutherland chatting with his receptionist in the waiting room. As she stared out the window, he looked up, their eyes met and he did not smile.

Please don't. Please don't look like that.

She paid the driver and reluctantly left the warm shelter of the cab. She entered the clinic and followed her expressionless doctor into his office. He sat down at his desk, opened a file and began reciting results.

"Well, your hemoglobin is up. That's good, isn't it?"

She just stared at him.

"Sugar was normal," he continued, "And you tested negative for HIV. So that's good, and also, your hemoglobin was a little low, but as I've said, improved. Yes, I did say that, that's right, and you tested negative for chlamydia and herpes."

He didn't pause; nor did he smile. As he looked up again, she wondered if she had heard him correctly. His eyes looked as though they were made of glass, like a doll's. Julie managed to say, "Negative for HIV?"

"Yes," the doctor answered. "That was the result you wanted, wasn't it? My guess is that your fellow didn't infect your friend. You said her husband was from Africa, didn't you?"

Julie nodded.

"Yes, my guess would be that is who she got it from."

Julie thought, *I love this man.* She wondered about his strange, reserved manner. Maybe he loved her too. How shy he was. Sud-

66

denly a picture appeared in her head of Paul as a toddler, trying to carry a bar stool from the kitchen to his bedroom for no apparent reason. She laughed at herself. Then, repeating Dr. Sutherland's last sentence to herself, she laughed with relief. She laughed out loud, and ignored his blank stare and complete silence.

When Mike arrived home that evening, Julie was waiting in the doorway, bursting with her happy news. Only slowly did he meet her eyes, acknowledge that he understood what she was telling him. His expression remained grim, unforgiving and terrified.

"It doesn't mean anything," he said as he brushed past her. He was about to retreat into his bitter silence, but seemed to change his mind. He turned and explained wearily, "We have to wait until a year after the... the last time."

Julie knew that if she told him again that it had been a short affair, and that they had used condoms, it would be of little comfort. She understood that, much like herself, he had been obsessing over the risks, though minuscule, of HIV cells touching the inside of her mouth, landing on a tiny, invisible cut, invading her, then easily crossing into his body. He had never used a condom. She realized now that he had never doubted her fidelity. Her innocence.

Julie told Mike that the doctor thought Max was negative.

"Oh really?" Mike said. "Is he a doctor or a clairvoyant?"

That night, after Mike had gone to bed, Julie tried to call Max, but there was no answer. She called again the next morning. This time, the phone rang only once.

"Have you heard yet?" she asked as soon as she heard Max's voice.

"No. You?"

She told him.

"That's wonderful," Max answered, but his voice was very subdued.

"But don't you see? It means you probably are too."

Max agreed, but without enthusiasm.

"In fact, my doctor thinks it was probably Lionel who infected

Patty," Julie said.

There was a silence. "I'm sorry. I guess that sounded callous."

"Why? Why would your doctor think that?" Max said, in a voice that was something just short of anger. He told her, not for the first time, that Lionel claimed he was negative.

"Well, because Lionel is African."

Max considered that for a few seconds.

"Well, that's pretty racist," he shouted into the phone. "So all Africans have AIDS, and they are all liars too."

A minute after they hung up, the phone rang.

"Hello, that is Max here again. You know what I am thinking?" His voice was quiet and sad again.

"No, what?"

"Angeline must have that disease."

The sentence came like a hammer blow. Julie felt as if someone had knocked the wind out of her.

"I mean," Max continued, "she is not really a very healthy kid."

He began to rattle off a list of health problems, from mysterious rashes to wheezing, to unexplained aches and pains, in a weird, dreamy, faraway voice. "This would fit your theor, of course."

Julie heard the accusation in his voice. She asked him if Angeline had been tested. He said he didn't know, and suggested she call Patty herself to find out.

"Oh, God," Julie said. "Patty must hate me."

"No, Patty doesn't hate anyone. She'd like that. She told me she'd like to talk to you, if you need to."

"If *I* need to?"

Julie felt a sudden rush of love for her friend.

That afternoon she had Paul safely buckled in his car seat and was reviewing the way to White Rock when she heard the phone. She ran into the house.

"Zo, I'm afraid it is bad news for me."

"No. No, Max, no. It can't be!"

"But you know," he continued softly, "about your result. That is really good. I am happy for you."

"How can you be happy about anything? And you know, I might still have it. I might have given it to Mike. I'll have to get tested again."

"I am sure you're all right. But listen, if I have given it to you, I promise I will shoot myself."

"Max, did you ever sleep with Ishl?"

"Ishl? Who is Ishl?"

"Your wife, apparently."

"Oh. What? No, that woman is a lesbian, Julie. Look, go see Patty. You need to talk to someone."

And she suddenly remembered Paul, strapped in his seat.

"Last night it got to be too much for me," Patty was saying. "So I howled."

At one in the morning, she opened her window in her little home above the chicken house, leaned out and howled at the moon. She tried to find solace now, in the humour of this scene, of a woman leaning out her window and making a crazy animal noise. But when Julie, paralyzed by her own fear, did not join in her laughter, she held her and broke down in her arms. Like a storm breaking without warning, big convulsive gasps, and both their blouses and faces were wet with her tears.

"I had a fever last night," Patty whispered into her ear, and then began to wail. "I don't want to have AIDS already. I don't want to die now."

Julie read a pamphlet called "Everything You Ever Wanted to Know about AIDS." It explained that the old Eliza test wasn't very reliable, and that it had been replaced by the Western Blot test. Neither were really AIDS tests, or even HIV tests; all they could do was detect the presence of the antibodies the body manufactured against HIV, and not the virus itself. The body could take months to manufacture those antibodies. When it did, if you were infected you might have a fever, a sore throat, or other flulike symptoms.

She was taking her temperature for the fifth time one scorching day in late August when her husband quietly packed a suitcase and left in a cab.

The phone rang. Paul moved towards it, but stopped and looked at his mother.

"What do I say," he asked, "if it's for Daddy?"

Julie gestured to him to hand her the phone.

It was Max. He told her that Patty was in the hospital.

"She has had some bad news," Max said, and paused. "And she's developed a brain tumour... and... she's saying goodbye to all her friends now."

Patty had read that people usually lived several years before finding out they were HIV-positive, and then, with pills, continued to live full, healthy lives...

"She can't be dying already," Julie said. *How ridiculous.* None of this could be happening. None of them were heroin users, promiscuous, or even gay.

"I think she can," he said softly. He told her he thought it was possible to die of a broken heart.

How absurd. Julie felt frozen.

"This is not your fault," she told him.

"No," he agreed, sighing.

Already bald and ghoulish in her hospital bed, Patty talked about the three things she used against dehydration: snow, ice and ice water. She didn't notice that her visitor was about to break down. Julie asked Patty how she was.

"Well, I'm dying," Patty said.

"Where are you going?" Julie surprised herself with the question that leapt past her lips.

Patty said she didn't know. "Hope somewhere where I'm not so thirsty."

Julie wondered if her visits with other people were more meaningful. Marjorie, an old high school friend of Patty's appeared, waving incense, chanting, and performing complicated hand signals over the sheets, from which Patty's large feet stuck out, somehow profoundly, unbearably poignant.

"You've got one foot in this world, the other in the next," Marjorie said. "It's a neat place to be."

Julie remembered what a nurse had told her as she entered the room, that Patty was high as a kite on morphine. Later, when Patty's beautiful doe-eyed sister Clara appeared, Patty cancelled the peace she had made earlier with her death.

"There's still a few good years in me," she said. Her voice was cheerful and strong, though her face, a perfect death mask, belied the truth.

A week later, a letter arrived for Mike from Ishl. Julie stared at the envelope, turned it over a few times and tried to read something, some intent, in the handwriting. She called Mike, who had moved to an apartment near his studio.

"Open it. Read it," Mike told her.

"It's for you."

"You're capable of sneakiness; you are capable of opening a letter and reading it."

"How is it sneaky if you tell me to?"

"It isn't."

"So… what's in it for you, if you can't hold it against me?"

"For once, I'll have some control over what happens."

"Shall I read it aloud?"

"Nah. I'll pick it up the next time I come by. Next time you need a babysitter." There was a sort of flippant bitterness in his voice.

"Okay." Julie said. "Paul wanted to know… "

But he'd hung up.

Julie braced herself for more pain. She slit the envelope open and unfolded the sheet.

Dear Mike,

I've been trying to call, but it's always either Julie or your kid who answers these days. I want to tell you that you should take this opportunity to do what you need to do. You can't waste your life denying your nature.

I guess I don't need to tell you to stay safe.

Take care,

Ishl

A month after Patty died, Max and Julie met at night, at their old café. They sat next to the door, by the window, watching the darkness and the rain, too sad to speak. After a few minutes, Max said that a friend of Patty's had run into some people who knew Lionel. It seemed that Lionel had told all his friends that his ex-wife had died in an accident while "driving a car with some bad people."

"I can believe he said that," Max added.

"Oh, I didn't realize you'd met Lionel."

Max said he hadn't, but that he used to live around the corner from the couple in Montreal. Julie suddenly thought of the man falling down the stairs next door. The flat cap.

"I knew some African friends of Lionel," Max said. "But no, I've never met—" He stopped, and then mumbled something that sounded like "my killer."

Julie looked at him.

"He died ten days after Patty, so what is the point of holding a grudge? It's just so African, you know, that kind of simple language. *Driving with bad people.*"

Julie's head was spinning.

Max told her that Patty's parents had already bought their plaques and their places in the cemetery, to be buried next to her.

Julie sensed there was more bad news coming, and she held her breath.

"Two and a half," he finally said, his voice breaking.

"Two and a half?" Julie repeated stupidly.

"Ya, they bought these three headstones, one for Angeline," he said, shaking. "I'm not supposed to tell anybody," he whispered as she enclosed him in her arms. He finally allowed himself to cry.

After a while, Max got up, went outside to smoke a cigarette. They sat, separated by a pane of glass, and stared at each other in silence.

"What was he thinking?" Julie said to Mike. "How could he do that? Knowingly infect his wife, impregnate her…"

"I can imagine what he was feeling," Mike told Julie. They were sitting at a card table in his apartment, drinking wine. Paul was asleep on the sofa. All the secrets had been laid bare. Mike looked slightly different. A smoother shave and a new shirt, louder than what he used to wear, unbuttoned at the collar.

"It's pride. It's not an African thing. It's a male thing. You can't admit you're vulnerable." In Lionel's case, he explained, he couldn't admit he was sick.

Six months later, Paul, Angeline and Julie stood at a crosswalk waiting for the light to change. Julie in the middle, holding their small hands. Angeline had a doctor's appointment at the hospital. The two children were quiet, apparently deep in thought. Angeline was the first to speak.

"You know," she started. "In movies, where there's bad guys, usually there's two working together, kind of."

Paul agreed, apparently on the same wavelength. "One is really fat, and the other is skinny."

"Or one is black, and the other is white," Angeline suggested.

"Or one's a man and the other's a woman," Paul said.

"And sometimes they fight a little bit," added Angeline.

"And it's hard to catch them," said Paul. "The police… They… The trouble is, they can't find them because they don't really act like bad guys. I mean, they do bad things, but they're not really, *really* bad."

"Or maybe they are, but it's just hard to see," said Angeline. "Or maybe they're mostly good but they do bad things because sometimes they just can't help it."

"Yeah," Paul and Julie agreed in unison. The light turned green and they crossed the street.

Something Steady

"Why *do* you wear a key around your neck, Mickey?" The way Sylvia asked the question, it was like she had already asked him the question and he hadn't answered. So why was she asking it like she was asking again? He was *sure* she hadn't asked, because he was paying attention and there was nothing wrong with his ears. He touched his ears briefly and shook his head. He focused on his thoughts, trying to remember *for sure*, the way his sister Ellie had always told him to. He frowned and thought. When he looked up at Sylvia again, there were other people's heads next to her, and they were all waiting for him to answer.

For example, there was Abby from the next cash, and there was James, who was a bagboy like him but not really like him because he went to college. And there were a teenage boy and two teenage girls waiting at the till. They were all smiling a little, so he smiled back too. Then he realized he had been thinking of *his* question, and his thoughts, and not Sylvia's question, and he didn't really know how to answer hers.

"I guess because Ellie says to. I guess I do most things because Ellie says to."

And he didn't mind, in general. He knew Ellie was smart. That's why his mother had told Ellie to look after him and not the other way around, even though he was really Ellie's big brother, and she was the little sister. He wasn't used to living on his own yet, and he sure wasn't used to having a job yet, but things would be fine soon. He wished Ellie could help him out with answering questions like this, the questions starting with *why*. But these days Ellie was really busy with her new husband, Kevin, because they had to start a life together, and that's why he'd had to go away.

"Who is Ellie, Mickey? Is that your girlfriend?" James was smiling, and so were Abby and Sylvia, but they were smiling behind their hands.

"No," Mickey said, and felt his cheeks burn. "Anyway, I don't lose it this way." He nodded at the other people before looking down again at the bag he was packing. There was a trick to it. Heavy things, like frozen fish, on the bottom. Eggs separate or on top of something steady. The frozen fish was pretty steady.

"What key is it, Mickey? Is it the key to your heart?"

Mickey stopped what he was doing and looked up. Sylvia was smiling. She had very nice teeth. The other people were smiling too, not just behind their hands. He smiled back. Sylvia was just kidding, he decided, and in a nice way.

"Naw," said Mickey. "It's the key to Mrs. Myers' house."

"Who's that, Mickey?" asked a teenager he didn't know. "Is that your girlfriend?"

The boy seemed to be a customer and a friend of Sylvia's at the same time.

Mickey turned to look at him, and then slowly at Sylvia.

"Her?"

"No, Mrs. Myers."

"Naw. Mrs. Myers is the lady who has the house. I have a room in her house. She makes me breakfast and supper. Sometimes she leaves a bowl of Cheezies on the table in case we get hungry other times. I think I am the only one that eats them, though."

"That's great. Is she cute?" the boy asked, but he didn't wait for an answer. Instead, he asked Sylvia what time she was finishing, and then the others, including Abby, started talking on top of each other about going to one of their houses. So the teenage boy and the two girls were customers *and* friends of Sylvia's, James's and Abby's too. Mickey wished he knew that trick, how to turn customers into friends.

The boy had a ring in his nose that reminded Mickey of the cow calendar on Mrs. Meyers' fridge. Mickey wondered what would happen if he suggested they come to Mrs. Meyers' house, but he also knew that his part in the conversation was over. He finished packing the bag. Potato chips, he remembered Mr. Markham saying, always went on top.

Kevin had got Mickey this job. They had driven over in Kevin's black sedan one muggy, drizzly night. Inside Markham's Groceries, everything was very bright, white and cold. Kevin told Mr. Markham that Mickey had a lot of potential. Mickey had wondered about the word *potential*, and had decided it was not like polenta, which was sold next to the white flour, in small, medium or large bags, next to where Mr. Markham had been standing. The bright lights were making Mickey's thoughts race around madly.

Kevin told Mr. Markham that Ellie, Mickey's sister, held him back. Mickey's mind flashed back to the car crash, Ellie throwing out her arm against his chest as the car lurched forward, his mother lurching forward too like when she had drunk too much, and how she had started to swear but had never finished her bad word.

Mr. Markham had a skinny neck, black hair and glasses with black frames. He looked a bit like a crow, he didn't say much, and he wasn't a big smiler, but he called Mickey "son" and Mickey liked that. Mickey had never known his father. He remembered his mother, but mostly all he remembered was that she liked to drink cider on the orange couch in front of the TV and that Ellie hated that so much that she had gotten rid of the orange couch, the cider and even the cider glasses after the accident.

Once Mickey started working without supervision, he rarely

77

saw Mr. Markham. He spent most days with Sylvia, or sometimes with the other girl, the one who was pretty like Sylvia but didn't seem to enjoy talking to him. Her name was Sandy, and Mickey wondered if she was called that because of her sandy hair. He had tried asking her that once, but she just looked at him blankly, and then at her watch. Then he had told her that Kevin had taught him how to read the time, but not on a digital watch like hers. She hadn't said anything to that either.

At 6:15 Sylvia counted the cash and a few minutes later they went outside. Mickey hung around while Sylvia locked up. He offered to walk her home.

"No, not tonight, thanks, Mickey. I'm going over to Julian's."

"Okay," said Mickey. He knew the boy's name now. But he doubted he would ever see the inside of Julian's house. Something hurt under his ribs. He wondered what would make him feel better. He wondered what was for supper at Mrs. Myers' house.

Sylvia gave him a little wave and crossed the street. Mickey continued down the same side, past the hardware store, the pharmacy and the beginning of the long row of skinny houses. A woman was walking back and forth from the beginning to the end of the row just like she did every day. It was the little woman who called him Michael. She had thin grey and red hair that poked out of a red headscarf, a brown cardigan over a red t-shirt, a brown skirt that looked itchy, and thin grayish legs. Mickey thought she looked like a robin.

The woman stopped in her tracks as he approached and then moved closer to him and peered right up into his face. Her eyes were very large for her face, and a very bright blue. Her face, a warm nut-brown, seemed to crack into little lines when she smiled. She opened her mouth and cried, "Michael!"

Mickey thought of correcting her, but he actually liked being called Michael. Before, when he went to school in the special stream, the kids in the normal stream would say, "Hey, Mickey, you sure your name isn't Goofy?" and he kept getting in trouble for punching, for *not using his words*. If he could have been Michael then, maybe school would have worked out.

"Michael," the woman was saying. "You don't be late for supper now. You don't like it cold, and neither do I." She walked into her house, letting the screen door swing shut behind her.

Mickey stood there for a minute and then continued down the street. He looked back a few times, wondering if she would come out again. He wondered what she was making. Mrs. Myers was the one who was supposed to be making him supper. Mickey came to the tiny store with the snacks and the magazines with the naked girls and then to the little bridge that led to the hill that went down, and then the street that turned into Mrs. Myers' street.

A small child toddled by, led by the hand by his mother. Mickey pulled the string from around his neck and began to open the door with his key. "Right, left, click." The little boy craned his neck around to stare at Mickey. Mickey felt stupid; he had said the words aloud. He felt his face grow hot. As he was coming through the door he heard Mr. Dixon call out, "Here's someone who will eat your horrible muck."

Mickey stood at the door with his head cocked. Mr. Dixon hadn't said "idiot" or "retard" this time, probably because the last time Mickey had lunged at him and Mr. Dixon had been forced to apologize. Mickey had felt very tall and wide next to Mr. Dixon.

Mickey walked past the kitchen, and quickly looked in. Mrs. Myers was just standing by the stove, looking at Mr. Dixon. Mr. Dixon was pushing his plate away and standing up. Mickey ran up the stairs to his room, sat on his bed and looked around.

Ellie had oohed and aahed about the room. She had said the colour was pretty. Robin's-egg blue, she'd called it. The bed was covered with a bright yellow bedspread that she called a happy sort of colour, but Mickey missed the one he'd had at home, with the Simpsons faces and the smell of Oliver, their basset hound. There was a framed picture of him and Ellie when Ellie was just his sister and not Kevin's wife yet. Ellie's hair was naturally curly then, and she wore braces. Next to her, Mickey thought, he just looked like a big fat goof. And he still looked the same, hadn't changed at all, despite being a big independent grown-up now.

He was hungry but he could already taste the warm salty water that was pouring down his face, and he knew he couldn't let Mrs. Myers see him being a crybaby. He heard someone coming up the stairs. The footsteps stopped at his door.

"I'm not coming down for dinner, Mrs. Myers. I'm not going to eat your horrible muck tonight."

Mickey clapped his hand in front of his mouth. His heart was beating very fast. There was no noise, and then the footsteps went back down the stairs.

Mickey felt awful and better at the same time. He wouldn't have pork chops now, but maybe he could find something else to eat. He had fifty dollars that Ellie had given him for emergencies. That was probably enough for several bags of potato chips at the little store across the bridge.

Sweaty and excited now, he wiped his tears and swallowed down the ones that had ended up in a snotty pool in his throat. He went to his closet and found his jean jacket, making a clanging racket with the coat hangers.

What's he doing now? Mickey heard Kevin's voice in his head, and wondered if he should be more careful. Making noise made him feel less lonely here, though. It helped fill up the quiet.

Anyway, he was going out. Maybe someday he would be the one with the girlfriend or the wife, and Mrs. Myers and Mr. Dixon would be the ones moving out. Could that happen? He puzzled over this as he left Mrs. Myers's house, yelling out one more time, "I'm not eating your horrible muck!" He slammed the door behind him and ran out the door.

He ran all the way to the little store, stopped and looked through the window at the young girl behind the counter. She was awfully pretty, and probably had nice titties too like the girls in the magazines. He wanted to go out on a date, he thought, but every time he'd asked a girl, she'd said no. He first asked a girl when he was fifteen and she'd said no. Then when he was twenty-six he'd asked another girl and she'd said no too.

At the store, he was putting six bags of potato chips and a six-pack of Sprite on the counter when a voice behind him said, "Are you having a party, Mickey?" He turned to see Sandy come in. He was confused for a moment, because at work, at Mr. Markham's, he had never heard her voice, or not talking to him, anyway. Behind her, a young man with a crewcut grinned at him as he grabbed Sandy by the belt loops and pulled her against his front. Did they think he was the one having the party?

No, because when he shook his head, they just started talking to each other and kissing as if he wasn't even there. After that, they didn't look at him again.

The pretty girl behind the counter didn't look at Mickey either, as she gave him his change and the case of Sprite, and stuffed the potato-chip bags into other bags. He figured that Sandy had been making fun of him, and tears started to fill his eyes again. He could hardly see as he took the change and stuffed it into his pockets. He hurried outside and started to walk back up toward the bridge with his snacks. Suddenly, he heard Sandy yell out, "Don't!" He wondered if she was talking to him again. Maybe she didn't want him to go away; maybe she wanted him to come to the party after all. "No, stop!" she cried out. She said something to the boy in a lower voice and they both laughed. Mickey was afraid to turn around. Maybe they were just messing with him. Finally, he did turn around and saw the boy with the crewcut grab Sandy around the waist and carry her. She was struggling and shrieking, kicking with her legs and also swatting at him with her handbag. Her shrieking filled Mickey's head with something very white and he ran back. He pushed the boy down so that he could kick him properly. Sandy popped out of the boy's arms. She was still screaming, "No, stop, stop it!" but her voice sounded even more desperate than before, so he kept kicking to make sure the boy with the crewcut wouldn't start up again. He kicked him in the stomach, in the legs, to make sure he stayed down, and then in the face, to stop him from shouting. The boy went quiet and his eyes stared and were kind of glittery. His face looked cute, like a girl's or a baby's, or a small animal's, but his mouth looked smashed open and was filling with blood, red as rose petals. He reminded Mickey of a squirrel he had seen once in the middle of a road. Ellie had said there was nothing to do about it. Sandy wasn't screaming anymore. She just sat on the sidewalk, holding her knees and rocking a little bit, and whispering "Yes," or maybe "Jess." She didn't look at him. It was like at work. He knew there was no use talking to her.

The sky was darkening with both grey clouds and nighttime. He suddenly realized that he had taken off his key when he'd come back from work and had forgotten to put it back on. He felt very tired. He wasn't sure he could go any further; he was like a car out of gas. He wanted to ask Sandy or anybody at all to push him along, but he wasn't even sure where he could go now. He went and collected his case of Sprite and his bags and walked to the bridge. He looked down at the brown water underneath. *I can't swim, but I can jump.*

Then he heard a woman's voice.

"Michael! Michael!" He ran across the bridge, dropping his bags, and almost bumped right into her. She looked up at him, bright little face, eyes like robins' eggs, and touched his cheek. "You'd better come in, now. Your supper is ready. Come in before it gets cold."

She turned and went into her house, letting the screen door slam shut behind her. Mickey looked at the pale orange light from her front window for a moment, then opened the door and followed her inside.

The Perfect Guy

Until Sue met the new owner of the Cookie Café in Gastown, she never came across anyone she wanted to date. She hardly ever met any single men, and the ones she did meet all seemed to be unattractive macho slobs, other women's cast-offs. But the first time she ordered coffee from Thomas, something stirred inside her, a small hope. He gave her a sweet smile. He was tall and gangly, had white streaks in his black hair. His haircut was a little odd, short back and sides with something like a small shelf on top of his head. He was soft-spoken, and when he whispered, "Two thirty-five, please," he sounded apologetic.

"That's okay," she heard herself say.

The second time she went to the café, a woman on stilts was standing outside, too tall to come through the door. The woman asked Sue if she wouldn't mind bringing her a cup of coffee. She threw down some change. She said she drank it black.

"Have you ever noticed that all the interesting people drink black coffee?" Sue asked Thomas, to break the ice.

"No," Thomas said, as he served her her latte in a ceramic mug. He told her he wasn't sure it was safe to serve coffee to someone on stilts.

Sue decided Thomas was a wise person. She liked that he didn't pigeonhole his customers according to the colour of their coffee. She decided he was the sort of person who thought things through.

"You're going to have to come down… Amy," she said to the

woman on stilts as she suddenly recognized her despite her theatrical makeup. Amy had called Sue to unblock a drain several times.

Sue's career choice had been made when she realized that her degree in social work would not help her change the world. On the other hand, she saw there was a need for woman plumbers, for women who were afraid of letting strange men into their homes. Most of her business came to her via word of mouth from other women. She could make her own hours so that she could be home when the kids arrived from school, and she liked the fact that she was meeting a need. But apart from the pain she lived with from folding her body under kitchen sinks all day—and the odours of rotting meat, urine, excrement and stagnant water—her biggest problem was that she hadn't met a nice man in a long time. She needed sex. Also, she wanted to meet a man so that her kids could have a decent male role model in their lives.

Someone other than, say, Jerry. Sue had to work every other Saturday to stay in business, because that seemed to be the day that most women needed help with blocked drains and broken toilets. That Saturday morning, Jerry had come to pick the kids up from her house. He let himself inside and was examining a photo on her mantelpiece when she walked into the room. As soon as she saw his smirk and heard him mutter to himself, she began to feel angry. Her friend Marc had sent it to her. They had grown up together in Nova Scotia, but she hadn't been able to fly to the East Coast for his wedding. The picture showed Marc and his new husband Phillip, in tasteful blue and brown suits, pants rolled up, barefoot in the tide line. The photo represented a triumph over a childhood of vicious bullying and years of subtle but painful ostracism.

As she got in her car that morning, she imagined what Jerry was muttering to himself. She was livid. She imagined herself throwing a pipe wrench in his direction. Or maybe she would just use her blowtorch.

Sometimes she got really mad at people, and felt they were responsible for everything that was wrong with the world. Nobody realized this about her because she didn't make a lot of noise. She bristled, which was something you had to be listening for, like snakes in the grass. She knew she couldn't do anything about Jerry's attitudes. It depressed her that they were so prevalent, and that there was a chance her own children would take them on.

My snake, she remembered, and ran into the house again. The boys had woken up, and had just run into the living room to give their father a hug around his waist. She wanted to tell them to cherish that moment; she was sure Jerry would be the kind of father who would discourage affection with his sons as they grew older. Most men were like that.

Sue went back to the café several times to see the man who seemed different. Thomas stood behind the long wooden counter, framed by a red brick wall. Neo-folk music played softly. Sometimes, jazz. He was a snappy dresser, a different retro cardigan and pair of pleated chinos every time. The co-owner, blond, conventionally handsome Cory, sported the simpleton look: a Cookie Monster t-shirt, faded jeans. Cory seemed too aware of his good looks, and was cool rather than friendly. Thomas, on the other hand, gave his customers genuine smiles. She wondered if he liked her too, if maybe they could fall in love. But something about the way he tilted his head sent her to her hairdresser's salon, a similarly stylish place just around the corner, to find out what was known about the new guy's sexuality.

"Oh, *we* know," Benjamin said. His client, a balding man with shaving cream on his head, turned around in his chair and smiled at her. The other hairdresser, Alan, laughed. They told her they'd all tried. And tried and tried. He was definitely straight.

"And single, dear," said the man in the chair. "Go get him!"

When she got home that day, she found that Pete, the unattractive macho-slob who lived downstairs, had left his hunting rifles outside on the back steps again. When she confronted him, he told her he was not responsible for her kids, that that was her job. He said to simply tell her kids not to come near his stuff. Then he tried to tickle her. He expressed surprise, and then anger, that she did not want to be tickled by him.

"Women love it," he insisted. "I've got the best hands."

She called her landlord, but there was no answer. She considered calling the police, but the idea made her feel exhausted. Instead, she walked over to visit her friends Sara and Elaine, cheerful half-sisters who had lived together for most of their thirty-something years. They were her size but wore their long wheat-coloured hair in buns on top of their heads, which made them seem taller. They weren't interested in her story about Pete. They wanted to know about Thomas.

"He's a snappy dresser," Sue said. "And he's really sweet."

"Well, *you're* sweet," said Elaine after a pause. Sue was wearing her work clothes: a black t-shirt, green overalls, a toolbelt. Sara and Elaine disappeared for a moment in the walk-in closet they shared and came back with a yellow dress for her to wear. They told her it was from the fifties. Sara called it a "frock;" Elaine called it "the magic dress." They also told her what to do: she had to go back to the café before the end of the week and boldly hold Thomas's gaze until he came over and talked to her.

"I love your dress," he said on Thursday as he walked to her table. "Is it linen?"

He told her they should go shopping together. Sue was charmed. She thought of her ex-husband Jerry, how bored and belittling he could be about the clothes she liked to wear. The only clothes Jerry appreciated were tops that revealed her breasts when she bent forward, or pants that were so tight she couldn't breathe.

She invited Thomas to a party at her house. She wondered if she should feel embarrassed. It was a small, rundown place near Commercial Drive furnished with second-hand Ikea junk. It smelled like a big wet dog, although she didn't own one. Her children and a few of their friends were having a great time tearing the stuffing out of the old cushions on the porch sofa, and pretending that it was snowing. She and her friends found it hilarious. She hoped Thomas would see it the same way. Maybe not, she suddenly worried, maybe it would make a bad first impression. She wondered how to stop it. She glanced at Jerry, who she had invited at the last minute, but who had been the first to arrive. He was on his third or fourth beer, and had a dopey smile on his face.

When Thomas arrived, in a suit jacket and black jeans, he told her that her house was *fabulous.* Jerry rolled his eyes. Sue introduced Thomas to the children.

"You people are awfully small," he said. "Are you really people? Or are you bugs? I don't mind bugs, as long as they don't bite. Do you bite? You kind of look like butterflies. But you sound like bees. Should I be scared?"

The kids were shy, but friendly, and giggled at his awkward attempts at humour. Thomas looked at Sue and said he approved of her eyeliner. She blushed. She'd only put on a touch of makeup and didn't expect it to be noticeable. She told herself not to care. *Linen, liner, what's the difference?* she scolded herself. *It's good that he notices!*

Later that evening she spotted Jerry sitting on the back steps with Pete. When Jerry had arrived, Sue had mentioned the guns. Jerry was nodding at something Pete was saying. At one point he picked up a rifle and squinted through the sights. He said, "Bang!" not to Sue, but to Elaine, who had sat down on the grass across from the two men and was fiddling with the pins in her hair.

Thomas was standing next to Sue, watching this scene. Sue apologized for not having offered him a drink. He told her not to worry about anything, and added that everything seemed great.

"On the surface, anyway," he added, laughing.

"Yeah, everything is great except I have a dangerous maniac in my basement," she said.

"Don't we all," he said.

She looked at him and he bared his teeth. Then he stuck his tongue out at her.

The next day, her kids told her that Thomas was a lot like one of the teachers at their school, Patrick Carr. Patrick Carr was the kind of person Sue's hairdresser would call a raging fruit loop. "I think it's his neck," the older boy said. "Or something about the way he moves it," her younger son said. "And his voice. It sounds like the tinkly high notes on a piano." Sue was relieved, remembering that the boys liked Patrick very much; his computer class was what they lived for at school.

Sue's friends asked her where her new guy was, wasn't he supposed to come to the party? Yes, she told them, the guy you'd never met before, that was the new guy. They thought and thought. Finally: "You mean the gay guy? You're dating a gay guy?"

One day, there was an invitation on Sue's answering machine from Thomas to go on a camping trip the following weekend. When she told her friends about it, she pointed out that it was a rugged sort of offer. None of the gay guys they knew had ever enjoyed the great outdoors. But then, Thomas wasn't gay. And anyway, she didn't like camping either. None of that proved anything.

"They're all different," Sara insisted. "Like snowflakes."

"Who are all different?" Sue asked.

"She means gay people," Elaine said.

"No, I don't. I mean everybody," said Sara.

"You said 'they,'" Elaine reminded her.

On the phone Sue didn't tell Thomas that she disliked camping. She didn't tell him that sleeping in a tent wasn't the greatest thing for her back, and that she had only ever done it for the kids, who would be away at their dad's that weekend.

"I wonder if we could do it when my boys would be around to enjoy it," she said instead, but he sensed something and told her that first, he wanted to change how she saw camping forever. He would treat her like a princess. (She wondered if she heard or just imagined the lisp.) They could go with the kids another time, but he wanted to assure her that she would be comfortable camping for the first time in her life. She would be in the lap of luxury. His nervousness was making him say odd things, but she was nervous too. The word *lap* made her blush. They hadn't gotten close to the subject of laps. Just one quick peck on the cheek after the party. That's all that had happened.

The night they left, Sue dropped the kids off at Jerry's. Although he ate, drank and dressed like a slob, he lived in an apartment in the West End filled with expensive black leather sofas and love seats. He had just bought a second flat-screen television. When she got there, he was on the phone discussing pizza with a friend. There was a DVD of *Cars* on the chrome coffee table. She supposed that was his plan: the kids would be entertained with some crap for two-year-olds while he and his buddies watched some stupid game. She was preparing what she was going to say to him when he looked up from the phone and asked her who she was going camping with. When she told him, he looked puzzled.

"By the way, you don't have to worry about Pete's guns any-more," he said after a moment, surprising her. She realized she hadn't seen the guns for a week or so.

"Oh, thanks, Jerry," Jerry said to himself, and then added, "No problem, Sue."

"Wait, what do you mean? What did you do with them?"

"Nothing. I just told him if I ever hear that he's left them out again I'll come right over and shove them up his ass."

"All of them?"

"Oh, thanks, Jerry. No problem, Sue," Jerry repeated. He was wearing a wife-beater, and the hair hanging down from his armpits seemed longer than she remembered. She felt a rush of desire for him, and told herself to stop it, to push it down.

Thomas picked her up in his van. It looked very battered, and there were empty pop bottles rolling around. She wondered if Thomas was a slob too, just in a different way.

At the first intersection, a couple of yahoos in the next lane shouted something at Thomas, something about his haircut.

"Hey, it's Kramer! Hey man, it's Kramer! Get a load of his hair!"

She turned and looked at him; his face was tense and he didn't respond. She wanted to defend him, but realized it might make him feel worse. Still, if she had been wearing her plumber's gear, she realized, she would have shouted something out the window. Something about those clothes made her feel strong. When the light turned green, the other car stayed next to them, two of the passengers leaning out of the window, jeering and cackling. A picture appeared in Sue's mind of Jerry looking into the sights of Pete's gun.

They lost the yahoos after three intersections.

They drove to Horseshoe Bay, took a ferry to Vancouver Island, and arrived at the beach at eight in the evening. It was only April; it was raining and cold. Thomas was well prepared, though, with Mountain Equipment Co-op sweaters and jackets. Sue wanted to know if some of these clothes once belonged to another woman, but couldn't bring herself to ask.

"Isn't this great?" he said. "The air is just so fresh and invigorating!"

She told him she thought she had seen a sign that said no camping until June. He assured her that they were trespassing, but nobody checked, because nobody did this.

"Except me," he added. "And now you."

He told her that his friends weren't interested in camping at this time of year, and he hadn't had a girlfriend in ten years. Sue felt him feeling her stare at him.

"It's been eight since I even slept with a woman."

He said this as if it were commonplace, as if he were ninety-eight years old, rather than only thirty-eight. She felt sad for him, but realized he didn't look sad. He was self-contained, she decided.

That was what gave him the courage to be different.

Still, a shiver ran up her arms. If he dated so infrequently, then this little trip had to represent an enormous risk on his part. And she wasn't sure how she felt about him yet. Her feelings seemed very beige and grey. She wanted them to match his, which were some other, brighter colour. She reminded herself to live in the moment. Concentrate on this place, completely desolate, at first glance, a place of different shades of brown and grey: sand, driftwood, seaweed, pebbles, rocks, rainy sky. But then there was the polished peachy pink of the seashells, the gold of a starfish, the brilliant black of mussels clinging to the gleaming wet rocks, the blue and silver of the water. And now here was Thomas, running up behind her and hugging her from behind. He kissed her neck. There was nothing tentative about the gesture. But the rough, rocky landscape seemed to contrast with and highlight his lack of masculinity: the air was rank and salty, but *he* smelled pretty. He was very clean-shaven. Maybe tomorrow he would be bristlier. Jerry was never clean-shaven, and he smelled...organic, she remembered. He had a *body* smell. As Thomas kissed her throat, she thought of Jerry with the gun, talking to Pete and to Elaine, Elaine's golden hair, her bare legs. Jerry in the wife-beater, dark clumps hanging from his armpits. She opened her eyes wide and blinked, trying to shake her ex-husband from her thoughts. Thomas stopped kissing her and asked her if she was hungry.

There was a windstorm, and its volume and force were steadily increasing, but Thomas was undaunted. He showed her how to collect the mussels clinging to the wet slippery rocks, and then how to eat them. The wind died down, the sky cleared and soon afterwards there were a trillion twinkling stars. Thomas deftly set up the tent, a large, luxurious red one equipped with a fancy air mattress, expensive down-filled comforters, brightly patterned pillows and cushions worthy of a harem. She imagined her sons bouncing around inside, wrecking everything. She missed them. She was filled with guilt, and a lot of it, she realized, was about Thomas, for whom she had yet to feel the slightest twinge of desire. He invited her to lie down, then crawled in the tent himself and abruptly pinned her arms down, beaming into her face. She finally relaxed and smiled back.

"Did you think I was gay?" he asked in his gay voice.

"What?" She felt her smile go away.

"Oh nothing. Lots of people think I'm gay when they first meet me."

With that he competently undressed both of them under the comforters. She wasn't aroused, but she tried to fake it. He did everything right. She wanted to respond, but she felt like a spectator, hovering over the bed.

"This is the first time," he said afterwards. "Sometimes it takes a few times."

So he knew. She scolded herself for being a bad pretender. She squeezed his arm and rolled over, suddenly sleepy from the fresh air.

In the morning he woke her up by reaching a hand inside the flap of the tent from outside and stroking her hair. She realized she had been dreaming that she was with Jerry. She felt enraged with herself. Thomas withdrew the hand, and, a few seconds later, put a cup of coffee next to her pillow. Then the hand came back and there was a wild rose next to her cup. Things Jerry would never have done.

But there had never been time. They had spent their years together bickering and making up and making babies. Until one day Sara told her that he regularly flirted with her and with other women and hinted that he was moving out soon. Jerry refused to defend himself. Sue told herself at the time that she didn't want to hear his side of the story anyway. Whatever he had to say would hurt too much.

Sue got up and joined Thomas, and they walked along the beach. The sky was grey and there was a thin low cloud of mist, like a film of skim milk. When Thomas began to talk, his shy voice was hard to hear over the screaming seagulls.

"You know," he said, "Cory couldn't believe that a pretty woman like you would be interested in me."

"And not him," they said at the same time.

"What a jerk," Sue said.

"Hey, he's my friend!"

"He looks like a Nazi."

"Hey!"

She told him he was too nice for the world and gave him a hug.

They drove home that afternoon. In the evening he left while she picked up the kids. When she arrived at Jerry's, he was scraping plates and putting them into the dishwasher. He helped her load the boys, who were both tired and whiny, into the car. As soon as they were settled in their car seats they fell asleep, as if their parents had flicked a couple of switches off. It was a chilly evening, but Jerry and Sue both stood on the sidewalk for a moment, looking at their children through the car window. He asked her if she had a good trip. She told him it was great, and checked his face for jealousy. All she could see was a smirk.

She put the kids to bed at home. Later, Thomas snuck in. They lay under the blankets in her attic bedroom. When he asked her what she felt like doing, she hesitated. She wished she had a magic bed. She didn't want to disappoint him; he didn't deserve that.

"Are you reading a novel or a book of short stories right now?" he asked, to her relief. He suggested they take turns reading aloud. She told him he was every thinking woman's dream, a sensitive man with an interest in literature.

However, after several pages of hearing him lisp through *Wuthering Heights*, she knew that the next day, before the kids woke up, she would have to dump him. She went to sleep sick with disappointment, guilt and dread. She could skip brushing her teeth, she thought, and wear something that smelled like her job.

Then it would be his turn to feel relieved. But she remembered his dating record and realized nothing would soften the blow.

"Oh well," he trilled the next morning, when she told him. He smiled and shrugged. She knew he was trying to spare *her*. They shared an honest look. His smile disappeared, and then he did. And that was all.

Jerry dropped by that evening, after the kids had gone to bed. Sue saw the reflection of a car's headlights streak across the wall of the living room and heard wheels crunch up her driveway. She watched him get out of the car and walk toward the back of the house. Sue went to the kitchen window and watched him glance down at the back steps. She knocked on the pane. He looked up and met her eyes. She went outside and stood in the backyard with him.

"Thanks," she said.

"Like you really have to worry about that asshole. You've got a blowtorch, for fuck's sake."

After a moment, he asked her how her back was.

"What do you care about my back?" she said, and then added that it was sore.

"That's what you get for sleeping in a tent," he said. "But you're always sore."

He turned her around and began to massage her back. She imagined his triumphant smirk. She didn't like being massaged standing up. It was uncomfortable.

"You rub me the wrong way," she said. "You've always rubbed me the wrong way."

"That's not how I remember it," he said as he turned her back around to him and dropped his hands to her bum.

"I knew you didn't really care about my back," she mumbled, without offering any resistance, leaning into him. "Speaking of assholes."

He didn't understand that she was joking. He stormed off, disappeared around the front of the house. She stood there as a cold breeze swept along her arms. She listened as he got into his car. She heard his car pull away. This was followed by a chorus of crickets and a dog that barked twice and stopped.

Two months later she ran into Thomas at the supermarket. He averted his eyes. When she said hello, he barely answered. She was pushing her children in the shopping cart, even though they were too big for this, too heavy for her to push. The wheels kept getting stuck. She was just so tired. What she really needed, she thought, was someone who would push.

Madison's Bag

By the time Sophie and Al finally got in the car, their daughter Kayla and her best friend Madison had been in the back seat for some time, waiting to be taken to an outdoor Beatles tribute concert. Their son Sam stood at the front door of their home in Longueuil and waved at them. They imagined Sam was relieved to have the house to himself, a treat for a teenaged boy. They waved back. Madison blew him kisses, and he seemed confused about how to respond, raising his hand to his mouth and then quickly withdrawing it. His embarrassment made both Madison and Kayla erupt into giggles.

"Your brother's hot," Madison said, not bothering to lower her voice.

Just as Al was starting the engine, Madison's parents surprised them by suddenly appearing beside the car. They lived a few blocks away.

"Sophie, take this!" Madison's mother, Jane, said, crouching next to the window and tapping on the glass. She thrust a folded white paper bag into Sophie's hands. A vacuum-cleaner bag? Sophie was confused.

"In case she has too much to drink. For the way back in the car," Jane added, winking. Her husband Frank winked too.

The girls were barely fifteen. Sam had just started to drink alcohol the week before, at his high school graduation. But then, he was athletic, maybe even a bit of a health freak. He swam or jogged every day and he was always playing two different team sports at any given time. There was something simple, self-contained and wholesome about him. His hair, his eyes and his tanned skin all different hues of golden brown, of whole grains and honey. Sophie turned around and looked at the girls. They were sitting in the back seat sharing an iPod. Madison gave Sophie a winsome smile. Kayla's eyes were closed and her chin was bobbing to the music. They both wore cut-offs and t-shirts. Madison's shirt featured a striking scene from the Second World War: a mother, distraught but brave, handing her child over to someone on a train.

"Are we naïve?" Sophie asked Al.

He shrugged, and glanced in the rearview mirror.

She asked him if he would get drunk when he was their age.

"Not with my friends' parents, I don't think," Al said.

She put the bag in her lap and examined it. It was an official vomit bag, the kind you get on an airplane. Jane and Frank travelled a lot.

The concert was a small, local event in a park in St. Hubert. There were about three hundred people there, most of them much younger than Sophie and Al, but older than the girls. They stood and watched the band. The musicians were convincing; they could have been mistaken for the real Beatles. Sophie and Al didn't dance, but they swayed a little, and clapped politely after each song. Madison whooped and whistled when they began to play "Day Tripper" but soon got bored and left after whispering something in Kayla's ear.

Sophie asked Kayla where her friend was going. She shrugged. She seemed more interested in watching the show. Sophie watched Madison cross to the refreshments stand. Instead of going to the end of the line, she butted in up front and began to chat with two men in baseball caps. From where Sophie was standing, it was hard to tell their age, but apparently they were old enough to buy beer. When their turn came up the young woman behind the counter placed some bottles on the counter and took their money. Sophie couldn't see how many bottles. She tried to follow Madison's movements, but some bodies blocked her view and then she couldn't see her anymore.

The singer's mike died as he began to sing "Help!" and he tried to get the soundman's attention. The soundman was checking his phone. Sophie considered Madison's parents and their vomit bag, and tried to convince herself that if they weren't concerned, then she shouldn't be. Still, it would be a drag for Kayla if her friend spent the evening getting hammered. She looked at Kayla. She was definitely into the polite-looking boys on stage.

The sound returned to the singer's mike. The group moved on to the next song in their set, "Hey Jude," and Madison returned in the middle of it. For the first time, Sophie noticed the dark-green powder on her lids that made her appear beautiful, sad and sinister all at once. Madison ran up to Al and shouted, "Kayla's father, I don't know you but I think I love you."

She turned to Sophie. "You too, Kayla's mother."

Madison suddenly hugged her. Sophie could feel her bubble bra. Her hair smelled of cigarettes but also baby powder. As Sophie broke the embrace, she held Madison at arm's length and pretended to notice her t-shirt for the first time.

"That's quite the t-shirt," Sophie said. "Where did you get it?"

"At the drama-queen store," both girls said, and laughed.

Madison insisted it was true. "That's what the store's called. It's in New York."

"And it's where drama queens shop," added Kayla.

"My mother's a psychiatrist, and she says I'm histrionic," Madison said with disarming honesty.

"What impeccable pronunciation," Al said.

While they were driving home, the girls asked if Madison could sleep over.

It was late, and Sophie didn't feel right about waking her parents to ask for permission.

"I already texted them and they texted back, look," Madison told her. She leaned forward as she passed her phone up front. Sophie caught a whiff of beer on her breath.

Sophie looked at Al. He shrugged.

Kayla had a single bed and a hammock in her room. They supposed one of the girls could sleep in the hammock.

Sophie woke up in the middle of the night. She thought she heard voices in Sam's room. She went back to sleep and dreamt that they had a lot of houseguests, and that they were all slobs, especially Paul McCartney. In the morning, on her way out of the bathroom, she saw Sam's door open. Madison emerged, behaving as if she were blind and unable to see her friend's mother standing there. Or as if they were both blind. She crossed the corridor quickly like a small animal and disappeared into Kayla's room.

Over supper that evening, Sophie asked her kids what was going on.

"We were just talking," Sam insisted.

Al tried to catch Sam's eye by making ridiculous faces, but he ignored him. Kayla stared at her mashed turnips as if fascinated by them. She used her knife to turn them over as if looking for something underneath.

A few minutes later, Jane called and spoke to Al.

"Uh-oh," said Sophie.

"Just a minute, I'll ask… I'll ask Sophie," Al said. "Yes, ha ha, it *is* Sophie's choice." He put his hand on the phone and looked over at his family. "She wants to know if it would be too much trouble if Madison spent Labour Day weekend with us. They're going to Venice."

"For the *weekend*?" Sophie asked.

Kayla glared at Al. She turned to her mother and gave her an imploring look. Sophie shook her head at Al. It was Sam's turn to study his vegetables.

"Yeah, I… I guess this isn't going to work out, actually," Al said into the phone, swinging his head from side to side. His expression vacillated between a wide, simian grin and an uncomfortable grimace.

Later that evening, Sophie and Al returned from their walk to find Sam in the living room, asleep in an armchair, a slight smile on his face. He was hunched down and his legs were spread wide. On the side table next to him was his phone. Al picked it up and showed his wife the words on the screen: *I want to rip that preppy shirt off you. With my teeth.* Al tried to show her something else, something between Sam's legs, but she turned and went upstairs.

For the next few months, Sam spent each night waiting for a text. After he read it, he would leave. Sometimes the text came long after his parents went to bed; the sound of the front door closing behind him always woke his mother up. The next day his neck would look as if it had been attacked by a vicious bird. Sometimes, the text didn't come, and he left the house anyway. They could just tell. His nervous anticipation, his frustration, his agony, his longing, they all had a way of affecting the air in the house.

One night he came home sheepish after only half an hour.

"Drama-queen store closed?" Al asked.

"Yeah, well, the opening hours are a little irregular," Sam said.

There were periods of this, and then it would completely stop. In between, Kayla and Madison would sometimes get together, but Kayla gradually acquired new friends. Al took Sam to the doctor at one point because he was convinced that his night sweats and weight loss meant he had TB. Once Sophie thought she saw Madison walking downtown with her arms around a boy she recognized as one of Sam's friends. But they brushed past her quickly. She couldn't be sure.

Sam finished CÉGEP. He could have gotten into any university of his choice, but he chose a local one and continued to live at home.

His parents weren't sure how they felt about that, especially as he fumbled along, barely passing some of his courses. Smoking pot replaced the jogging and swimming. They would ask about sports, and he would say he'd missed the date to sign up, or his registration cheque bounced, or he forgot to go to the tryout.

When he passed his probational year, they were so relieved that Sophie thought of throwing him a party. Kayla was turning eighteen, and she asked her what she thought of the idea of a joint celebration.

"Sure. Who should we invite?"

Sophie suggested they could start with family, then add friends.

"You guys, of course," said Kayla. " And Grandma, Aunty Janice and her new boyfriend, what's his name?"

"Batman?" Al suggested.

"That's right, Wayne," Kayla said.

She didn't bother writing any of this down.

"Friends?" asked Sophie.

"Mika, Cassie, Madison. Oh wait," Kayla stopped and chewed on a cuticle.

Sam still sometimes disappeared at night; the hickeys made an appearance now and then as well. They couldn't be sure it was Madison. Al pointed out there were surely "other piranhas in the sea."

"I guess Sam and Madison aren't an item these days?" Sophie asked Kayla. She made an effort to sound casual.

"Never," her daughter answered. "If you ask them, they never have been, never will be."

Sophie said that she didn't understand.

"Madison doesn't really do relationships," Kayla said apologetically, as if this were all her fault. They noticed Sam then, halfway down the staircase, listening.

"It's okay. Invite Madison. I won't come," he said.

"No!" Kayla shouted.

"Invite her, it's fine."

"You have to be there."

"All right. I'll come too. It's *fine*, Kayla."

At the party, Sam and Madison sat together at one end of the table but were quiet and polite, like strangers meeting for the first time. Even so, Al's mother asked Sam if Madison was his girlfriend. Sophie and Al held their breath.

"No, Grandma. She's a girl, and she's my friend. She's Kayla's friend too."

Madison didn't say anything. She wound a lock of hair around her finger.

"I can see that. I know she's a girl. I want to know if she's your girlfriend."

Al's mother's hearing problem simplified conversations and made them more awkward at the same time. Not to mention her lack of tact. Sophie wondered if a lack of tact was a kind of courage. She wondered whether, if she had been less tactful, she could have kept everyone safer.

"Are those false eyelashes you're wear—?" Al's mother asked Madison.

"Do you want some chips, Grandma?" Sam shouted, interrupting her. He pushed a bowl of purple corn chips across the table.

"What?" Al's mother exclaimed. "Some shit? Why would I want some shit?"

Sophie took Madison aside as she was leaving to ask her if she wanted to sign the card for Sam. The rest of them had already signed, under the words "Congratulations to Sam, our future graduate, whom we all love to the craziest degree." Madison read the card, and slowly shook her head.

"I'll make him a card some other time," she said. They were in the narrow passage by the front door. She looked at the door behind Sophie and then met her eyes.

"I'm sorry," Sophie said, and moved aside.

* * *

One afternoon as Sophie was hanging a wash out on the clothesline, Maria, their warm, round, elderly neighbour, called to her from her backyard. She told her that she had spotted Sam crying uncontrollably on a park bench the night before.

"I went over and I said, "poor baby." I had some chocolate in my purse but he didn't want it. He was really sobbing like a baby. I still remember when he was little."

Sophie couldn't find any words at all. What was he doing, crying in a park? In a park! Every cell in her body reacted. Everything tensed. There was real pain in her gut. She felt her jaw set and it scared Maria away, up her porch stairs, back into her house.

That evening Sophie suggested to Sam that he move to an apartment.

"Somewhere closer to school," she said. His university was in Montreal, after all. Several metro stops away. Sam didn't say a word.

Before Sophie joined the family at the table, she walked around opening all the windows to get rid of the earthy smell emanating from Sam's bedroom. As she sat down, she raised her eyebrows at her son.

"Sure, I could do that," he said quietly.

She wondered if anyone noticed what she felt happening to her. She felt as hard as concrete. But also as potentially crumbly.

There was a silence. Then Al, in his jolliest voice, asked Sam about women.

"Women," Sam gave him a wry smile as he repeated the word back to him. He coughed and laughed alone, for a good twenty seconds. As if this were hilarious, the idea that there had ever been more than one.

"Madison has, like, an eating disorder, but with boys," Kayla told them one day. "She plays with them until she gets sick of them, stops, wants more, stops. But no... she's not sick. It's just what she does. That's her bag." Sophie could tell her daughter was determined to leave out the judgment.

"Her *bag*. It's touching when you try to talk like us," Al said.

"I just wish she would leave my brother alone," Kayla added softly, almost to herself.

It was true, what everyone said: it went by very quickly. Kayla fell in love and went to live with her boyfriend shortly after Sam left. Sophie and Al had been empty nesters for a couple of years, but somehow it hadn't felt that way until that day as they were seeing their son off. He was leaving town. Al and Sophie were giving him a lift to the train station. He had decided to take a job in Ottawa. Working in an office, proofreading legislative bills. He needed something mind-numbing, because marijuana didn't work anymore. Sam told them that he just needed some time away from Madison. "I am thinking of it as taking care of my mental health." He was pale and bluish, as if bruised, but from the inside.

Sam told them that Kayla had thrown a goodbye party for him the night before and that Madison showed up, uninvited.

"She just showed up," Sophie said simply, exasperation mixed with awe.

"Well, yeah, I guess she heard about it and realized an invitation wasn't coming."

They were walking into the station. Sam's parents tried to carry some of his bags for him, but he wouldn't let them. Sam told them that he tried to avoid her all evening. "And I wasn't subtle. But she followed me around, from the kitchen to the living room to the balcony. I hid in Kayla's bedroom. She found me. I went to the bathroom. She was waiting when I came out. Back to the kitchen. All around Kayla's apartment." He turned his head clockwise, then counter-clockwise.

"What did she want?" Al asked, and nudged Sophie, who watched Sam's face.

"Oh you know, 'Why can't we be friends, blah, blah, blah.'" He sighed and jerked his arm away so that Al couldn't make a grab for his duffle bag as they went up a staircase. "I was gonna crash at Kayla's, since it's right around the corner from here. But then Kayla was caught off guard when Madison came up, totally drunk, bleating about how she had been planning to sleep there, how she was way too drunk to make her way back to the burbs."

"She still lives with her parents?" Sophie asked.

"Yeah. So anyway, I told Kayla it was okay, but she didn't believe me. She went into a kind of funk."

"She worries about you, Sam," Sophie said.

"She worries too much. I told her I'd just go home and get a lift from you guys to the station. This way we get to say goodbye properly. I *told* her it was no big deal."

But they knew that look, the look his sister saw. They had seen that pained expression for so long, on a face still so young, still just settling into adulthood.

They reached the train platform. As Sophie hugged Sam's thin frame, her mind flashed back six years to that photo printed on Madison's t-shirt. They put their son on the train, smiled bravely, and waved.

Indelible Markers

DAD AND ME

I always knew two things about my dad. One: he loved me more than anyone else ever could—*more than the moon and all the stars in the sky*. He thought highly of every little thing I did. He sent my poems to poetry contests; he let me draw in magic marker, the kind that doesn't smell like fruit and says *indelible* in big serious letters, on the walls of his office, calling my pictures his frescoes; he told me that I made him *so* proud that his heart was always *so* full that he thought it might burst, which made me worry about him. And two: he was completely insane.

My dad had begged my mom to have one more child. He had really wanted a daughter. *There are no guarantees. Just because we've got three boys doesn't mean the next one is going to be a girl.* I imagine her explaining this to him with all the patience she could muster. This was a problem for her, having babies, because she had to work, at a time when few women did. She had to work because he often couldn't.

But seven years later she agreed, and that is how I came to be.

When I say he was insane, I don't mean that in a fond, facetious sort of way. I don't mean he was fun or dreamy or unconventional. I am talking about the fact that he was a paranoid schizophrenic, and that when he stopped taking his pills, he had vivid delusions.

I'm interested, in a detached way, that I have clear memories of understanding that he was crazy, even as a young child, even though my mother observed the strictest silence about her husband's illness, even within the family, almost to the point of denial. I say "almost" because I remember being seven years old and watching my mother crush Stelazine tablets into his cup of coffee, and the ensuing argument between them when he tasted his bitter pill, imperfectly dissolved in the sweet coffee, and spat it back into his cup. I remember the half-melted powder on the surface of his cup.

I remember it as though it were yesterday.

I remember, one overcast day, walking home from school to find my dad waiting for me on the front steps of our house, an open newspaper in his hands. He inquired about my day, but he couldn't quite smile, and he was trembling. I asked him what he was doing home, and he ignored my question. Instead, he gave me the newspaper and asked if any of the faces in the photographs looked familiar, if maybe one of these people had followed me home. He gave me a black magic marker and invited me to circle as many as I wanted. He'd already started. He'd circled a photo of an RCMP officer. I looked through the newspaper, and hoping to make him smile, circled Richard Nixon and Henry Kissinger. Unfortunately, this only added to his distress. His eyes widened and filled with tears. He held the newspaper tightly and thanked me in the voice of a man who knew he was doomed. He didn't want to talk about it.

I asked my oldest brother later what our dad was doing home in the middle of the day, and he said that he had been fired. I tried to make sense of this. *Fired?* Like out of a cannon? *On* fire? Was he *on* fire? Like, inside his brain? Was that why his eyes were watering and his thoughts were raging? Was his brain full of smoke? I wondered if I could get fired. If I made myself say ridiculous things, could I stay home from school with my daddy? If I told stories, would he let me into his world?

The man on the yacht is waving to the boy and me. The name of the yacht is *Monachus-Monachus*, which translates as the Mediterranean monk seal, an animal seen on the islands of Alonissos and Zakynthos.

The boy and I are dressed almost identically, in dark shorts, sleeveless white tank tops and sandals that you can pick up at a stand by the docks in Piraeus. I am not wearing a bra today, having rinsed it and left it to dry on a clothesline at the youth hostel. He's carrying the same long, rough, white towel as me, rented from the front desk for 100 drachmas.

We don't know each other. The boy stands out here in a way I don't, with his fair skin, long, sunny curls and eyes the colour of restaurant mints. He's very slight for a man, but then he's really a boy, no older than me. I am nineteen. We've both stepped out of the youth hostel at the same time and are walking, for now, in the same direction. We wave back hesitantly at the man on the yacht and continue to walk past the docks towards the beach. We both look at the seagulls, the sailboats, the other yachts. The tide is coming in. The water matches the boy's eyes.

There is a bond between us, things we already know. Like this: we're both very hungry, but we're trying to save our money for a ferry or bus or train to the next place. Our official story is that we're travelling, learning about different places and cultures, but really we're just landing once in a while, skimming the surface. Looking for something to eat.

He wraps his towel around his tiny waist.

"Ye should do this too," he says. "Tae let yer han's gang free."

For scavenging? I think. I say nothing as he takes my towel from my hands and wraps it around me. "Yer awfy wee," he starts to say, when the man from the *Monachus-Monachus* calls to us.

"Come. Come here. Welcome." A local man, middle-aged. Lopsided grin, tired eyes under bushy black eyebrows. Once handsome. Loose blue shirt, longish straight black hair blowing in the breeze. There is, under the brine, a whiff of onions and rosemary. "Come, you see boat."

The boy and I glance at each other, wordlessly board the yacht, and follow the man down a few narrow steps into the cabin. The cabin is warm, dark and muggy. It has the wood panelling of a suburban basement back home. There are floodlights in the ceiling. There is a fire extinguisher in a narrow corner next to a tiny sink. A pot of simmering liquid, the source of the enticing aroma, sits on something that looks exactly like a toy stove. Above the fire extinguisher, there is a sign featuring the English word WARNING. I can't read the rest from where our host has motioned us to sit, on a sofa upholstered in leather, with small round cushions covered with cartoon cowboys. I look around for something Greek. Well, there is our host, Christos, black hair poking out of the top of his shirt. A gold chain, a gold watch, gold in his teeth. He crouches down, suddenly disappears behind a curtain in the corner by the sink. When he reemerges, he hands us each a glass of ouzo.

"You see seals? I take you tomorrow, yes? Very nice."

Ouzo, I think, is basically black licorice in clear liquid form. The Scottish boy (his name, it turns out, is Tom) listens politely as Christos talks about naval mechanics. Whenever Tom says anything, though, Christos looks at him blankly and then turns to me with a slight frown.

Christos serves us eggplant soup, olives and bread. We are both ravenous but puzzled. In Scotland, in Canada, people do not randomly invite passersby in for food. Tom keeps protesting, "Naw, ah couldnae. Naw, a'right, ta, jist a wee bit. That's awfy good o' ye."

Christos is clearly very rich, at least for a Greek, at least in contrast to us. So far he has not spoken of emigrating to Canada. He beams at us affectionately as he refills our glasses.

"How nice. Nice young love, beautiful boy and beautiful girl.

You are so lucky."

Tom tries to explain that we are not together. That we just happened to leave the youth hostel at the same moment, for a walk on the beach.

"Yes, how nice, two beautiful young people on love honeymoon, yes? You sleep here tonight?"

He pins us down with his sad dark eyes. We don't say anything for a moment, and then suddenly, out of the corner of my eyes, I spot a small, neat picture frame on the wall. Blue background, as in a school photo. A dark-haired girl, perhaps a high school student, smiling merrily, showing white teeth and dimples.

"Your daughter?" I ask, not hopefully.

"I have no family," Christos confirms glumly, but his body shifts a little as he prepares to tell us a story.

"Ech, I have nephew. This is lovely wife of my nephew. They visit before. Then only him, but he keep her picture here. Her name Despina, but I call her Persephone, because she only visit in the spring. But now no." He sighs heavily.

"Perrsephone, the goddess o' sprrring," says Tom.

I glance at him, impressed. He acknowledges this with a humble half-bow. Christos doesn't seem to have noticed his intervention, for he continues.

"Persephone, this is the goddess of spring. Hades, this is lord of the underwear. He take Persephone. Then mother of Persephone, Demeter, she want Persephone come back, so she say Zeus, tell Hades, let my daughter come back. But then, Hades make Persephone eat apple."

"The pomegrrranate," corrects Tom.

"Not an apple, this is the fruit with the many seed," Christos says, ignoring Tom.

"A pomegranate?" I ask.

"Yes, yes, I think. In Greek, poido. Po-ee-do."

"Po-ee-do," Tom and I repeat obediently.

"Yes, she eat the poido and why she must come back at the underwear for one-three of year."

Christos belches, heaves himself up from his chair and excuses himself as he leaves the cabin. We soon hear his heavy footsteps on the deck.

"Wh't he's tryin' tae say is the underworld," says Tom. "An' Hades wis a fuckin' rapist!"

Tom is playing with one of my hands.

We hear Christos clear his throat and spit.

"Grrreat!" Tom comments dryly.

"My dad does that," I say, for no reason at all.

"Is that right? Why, is thir anythin' wrong wi' him?"

"Probably. A lot." And I laugh as if I have said something incredibly witty.

"Naw, naw. Wh't ah mean is, is he ill?"

"I just think something is wrong with him."

Tom nods. He tickles my palm with a forefinger, and my hand closes up around it like an infant's.

"How come you know about Greek myths?" I ask him. He seems more attractive to me now. Not just a pretty face.

"An' how come ye dinnae? D'they no teach ye Yanks anythin' at the school?"

"I'm not a Yank. I'm Canadian," I say, and half-pull my hand away.

"Is that right?" His eyes glint with amusement. He seems much more masculine now that he is mocking me. He grabs my hand back and pulls gently on my fingers, one at a time, leaving a cool buzzing sensation in each. "So, d'they no teach ye Canadians anythin' then?"

"Yes," I say brightly. I think: I am drunk. And then I say, "They teach us French."

"Oooo-la-la," Tom exclaims, and we look up to see Christos standing in front of us again. Tom unlaces his fingers from mine.

"Ah, Tom, you speak French!" he says, as if this has cleared something up that has been puzzling him. He frowns, and then his body shifts into storytelling mode again.

"Maybe then you can explain a story to me now. It is French story, about a man he die, and he write in blood on the wall, *Omar m'a tué.* What mean, *Omar m'a tué?*"

He stares at Tom, but I answer for him, "It means *Omar killed me.*"

This story, much briefer, has the ring of truth to it. Who told it to him? A French couple that he invited onto his boat? Why is he telling it to us now?

Now he asks us again if we will spend the night. He insists on a tour of the two cramped bedrooms, his and then the guests', with their identical fake-oak king-size beds and night tables. The air is hot and stuffy, but the bed looks inviting after youth hostel bunks. I try not to think of the blood graffiti story.

"D'ye want tae bide?" Tom asks me when Christos disappears behind the curtain again to get more drinks. Tom bores into my eyes with his. He has long eyelashes like a contestant in a little girls' beauty pageant.

"Bide?"

"Stay the night," he says. His voice is light and teasing. He holds my eyes with his, as if this both matters a lot and doesn't matter at all.

"Do you?" I mumble, for I don't know. The ouzo is making everything seem at once blurry and sharply scented, like a thick cloud of perfume.

"Yer right bonnie," Tom says.

No one has ever said anything like that to me before. I want to say, "You're the one with the goldilocks and the pretty eyes."

"I ha'e a lassie at home in Scotland, but she goes wi'ither lads," he says, his eyes glistening sadly.

The sky has turned to dark-blue ink. I wonder what time it is. Will the youth hostel be closing its doors soon?

Christos comes back with the drinks and asks us if we would like to take a shower. "Hot water, very nice."

At the youth hostel, showers are 200 drachmas, and they're cold. Tom begins the "verrry, verry good o' ye," stammering, but Christos unwraps his towel from around his waist, hands him a plusher version and pushes him up the stairs onto the deck, into the shower stall.

Then he turns around and considers me, as I have followed them up the steps, somewhat wobbily. Christos is about my father's age. He smells like a father too, a mix of aftershave and tobacco. But the fathers I have known all seem beleaguered by an abundance of human company. Maybe because he is a bachelor, Christos seems completely insane with loneliness.

I think of the photo of Despina. How to avoid ending up like Christos, scaring people with desperation and crazy storytelling? This is why people get married and start families, I think. Because they know that otherwise there is a chance they'll end up like this.

Maybe I should marry Tom. I don't know him, but we would have pretty children. I see a pair with golden ringlets, holding hands. We would be safe, I think. There is safety in numbers. I listen to the waves outside, hitting the shore, and for a moment it is as if the noise is the sound of alcohol rocking around in my head. The inside of my brain, I think, is ouzo, rocks, fog, deepening darkness.

Now Christos turns to me and says, smiling a little questioningly, "You wan me to tell you something about your young man, beautiful Cassandra?"

I'm speechless. My name is not Cassandra.

"No? Okay, go to him. Go to your young man."

I suddenly fear that if I decline, he will claim the right to have me. Drunk and dizzy, I let him push me into the stall with Tom. Tom is naked. His wet hair seems very long. I let the shower drench my clothes as we stare at each other.

"Tom, who is Cassandra?"

"Eh?"

"Christos called me Cassandra."

"Is that so? Whit do ye ken?"

"What do I what?"

"What do you know?" he says, in a soft American drawl.

"Is that a question?"

He just looks at me. Finally, he puts his arms around me and draws me to him. I kiss him tentatively, he kisses me back and for a moment we stay entangled within the warm, wet sensation like suckling children. And then he pushes me away.

I step out of the stall, confused and cold now in my wet clothes, and wait for him. Christos hasn't left me a towel. I had thought he was hovering outside the shower, but now I hear the bouzouki music from below deck. He must be waiting for us in the cabin with more drinks. Will he expect us to dance with him?

Tom comes out of the shower, avoiding my eyes. Miserably, I pat myself dry with the damp towel he hands to me on his way out of the stall.

He pushes past me, and in a moment I hear him in the cabin.

"Naw, thanks a' the same. Verry good o' ye. We ha'e tae go. Naw, we cannae bide. Naw, the lass has tae gang back tae the hostel f'r her stuff, ye ken, or we'd surely bide wi' ye."

His voice is light, sing-song-y. I can imagine Christos' expression of disappointment and bafflement. I don't want to go back but Tom returns to where I am standing, shivering. Fierce again, he grabs my hand and marches me down the steps, muttering, "Say 'Thanks' tae the good man, w'll ye now?"

A few minutes later we leave the boat, still holding hands. We smile and wave cheerily at the Greek as he watches us with a drunken, hurt pout. As Tom drops my hand I feel my face relax into a similar pose.

"Whit did ye dae that f'r, eh?" Tom barks at me.

"What did I do what for?" I snap back. Suddenly we're bickering as if we have known each other two thousand years.

"Whit did ye egg me on f'r? Whit did ye egg me on f'r when ah telled ye?"

"Telled ye what?" I ask, dimly aware that I am mimicking his accent. If we were a long-married couple, and not just two drunken strangers, would I be doing the same? Probably, I answer myself dully.

"Ah telled ye ah had a lassie at home in Scotland, ah did. Ah did tell ya. An' aye ye had tae keep on eggin' me on. Y'r brazen, aren't ye? Wh't did ye think ye were playin' at back there? Wh't wis on y'r min'?"

And on and on. I clam up. I worry that he's actually guessed what I was thinking.

"Naw, y'r no' a Cassandra. Y'r one o' the Sirens fro' Sirenus Scopuli."

I think of a friend back home, who had a lot more experience with men than me, but always complained, "They make no sense. They're not like us, you know. The things they come out with. They might as well always be speaking Greek." I will myself not to listen to Tom. Still, I keep tuning in. At one point he is saying, "And an'ther thing, ah never kent a lassie who hud so little respec' f'r her father."

Persephone and Hades

Of course, what I had no idea of, back then, was just how many affable strangers would turn out to be complete madmen, some even uttering threats. How many guys would find me bonnie and charming and sexy and delightful—and never call. Run into them in the street and they would look away, muttering to themselves, as if offended, as if I had somehow polluted them by virtue of my existence. And how sometimes it would be me, being the hot and cold psycho. The fact I was never slashed to death, my blood coagulating into gruesome sentences on a wall, fills me with amazement when I think about it.

I've been wondering lately what must have happened to Christos. Is he even still alive? And Tom. He must have changed a lot by now. I wonder if he still has his hair.

I dreamt that our footprints, Tom's and mine, had hardened in the sand as if in cement, and we stood looking at them, I puzzled, he unsurprised. He turned and looked at me with a trace of a smile and gave a wry shrug. He didn't look like himself. He kept morphing between my ex-husband and a man who advertises gunk remover on TV. My father, who died ten years ago of lung cancer, smiled sadly at us from the yacht, waving two white towels, before disappearing inside.

Between Black and White

On that first day of school, someone from the tiny office downstairs brought me up to Mrs. Wingart's classroom. I looked in the doorway. The room was dark and cramped. The children were sitting in rows at small wooden desks with inkwells, not around tables as I had been used to. Most of the children were thin and dark-skinned, and most of the girls wore short curly pigtails.

"Say hello and welcome to the new girl from Canada."

"HELLO. Welcome to P.S. 26."

I felt tears form in my eyes and I bit my lip. No one asked me to say anything, so I stood in the doorway and waited. And then it happened: Dena's voice, deep for an eight-year-old's, rang out from the back of the room.

"Yo, everyone, that po' girl's never seen so many black folk in her entire life."

"Dena," Mrs. Wingart said tiredly. "Sit down and shut up." But then she smiled.

I didn't know what to do. I was never sure about smiling.

My new school was called P.S. 26. It didn't have a real name like my old one, Crestview Elementary School. I figured it was because the people in the Bronx couldn't think of a pretty place or a special person to name it after, so they stuck with something basic. The Bronx looked old and sad and in need of a paint job, and so did P.S. 26. My mother had explained that the people were poor here, and that it was rare for kids to have both a father and a mother, let alone parents who had jobs they liked and that paid well. My mother was a mathematics professor at Concordia, my father a civil engineer. Families in the Bronx didn't have the basics. *We* had a piano.

Yet before I finished third grade we left Chomedey, a suburb of Montreal where we lived in a two-storey house across the street from a sprawling park, and drove to New York. My father had a new job. My mother hadn't quit hers—she was on sabbatical—and we hadn't sold our house. My parents were giving New York a try, which is why we would go back and forth between the two cities for several years.

Having lived in a Jewish neighbourhood, I associated the sound of the word "sabbatical" with time off work for spiritual reasons. But we weren't Jewish; we were Indian. This meant that our home smelt like incense. That we sometimes ate food that other people, like my piano teacher or my dad's boss, refused to even try. That when my parents went out to a party, my mother would dress in clothes that made her look beautiful, colourful and weird at the same time, like an exotic bird. It meant that when my parents spoke to each other, it was in a secret language—they called it Punjabi, or sometimes Hindi—that they never used with me. It meant that their English sounded different from the way other people spoke it, and that they listened to a fluty-voiced singer named Lata on the record player.

And we had brown skin. And no friends. Or maybe that was just me. In Chomedey, my parents did go to parties with other Indians who spoke their secret languages. But I would stay home with a babysitter named Lou-Lou who had a blue-black beehive and false eyelashes, and who I'd decided I didn't like because she would never let me stay up and watch *The Carol Burnett Show*. Also, once she complained that my father was cheap and that made me want to hit her. I would lie in my bed, wretched with bitterness, fantasizing about slapping her face.

When we drove to New York our car was stuffed with suitcases and houseplants. The border police threw the plants in the garbage. They were very rude. They made my mother cry. I remember the pots being upturned, the roots like spindly hairs emerging upside down from the dirt, but mostly I remember being very surprised at how upset she was.

We arrived at our new address around midnight. The building was tall and white, and somehow looked like a plastic toy structure next to the smaller greystone buildings. The street smelled strongly of dog turds. My mother and I stayed in the car as my father emptied the trunk, bringing in the suitcases one or two at a time. When I finally got out, I checked the sky. It was grey. My brothers, who were much older and who had stayed in Canada, had warned me that the tall buildings would block out the stars.

The building smelled of pee and Lysol, and the slightly more pleasant odour of tobacco. There were two elevators. One arrived abruptly, the doors opened, and we got in. There was another person in it, a tall, skinny, dark-skinned teenager dressed in black. He didn't say anything as we entered, just looked up and watched the movement of the light through the numbers as the elevator began its ascent. I watched the whites of his eyes, which seemed very bright against his dark face.

Our apartment was 11E. My father had already dropped the suitcases off here but now we waited as he took out three different keys and turned each of the three locks. As soon as we stepped inside, a harsh sour smell burnt my nostrils. Inside, our furniture was crammed together amid stacks of cardboard boxes. I recognized the sofa with the gold flower pattern and the green corduroy armchairs, although they were turned on their sides, with their top legs up. They reminded me of the geometry exercises I always found impossible and upsetting.

My father was explaining about the smell. He said it was because the super's exterminators had come by. He said the super said it was

119

on the house. I didn't understand the way he was putting words together, what he could possibly be talking about, and suddenly I wasn't even listening anymore. All the bad smells seemed to have settled in my stomach and I thought I might need to throw up soon. It seemed impossible that he could be serious, that we were really going to live here. I wondered when my mother would say something, when the secret-language shouting was going to start.

The following week I started school. There weren't many trees on the way to P.S. 26, but there were a few, and I paused, took a deep breath and tried to hold it as I walked on, as long as I could, all the way to the next tree if I could. This was because my brothers had mentioned that the air in New York was polluted, and also that trees sucked in the pollution and exhaled clean air. Except at night, when they did the opposite.

I always got to school a little out of breath. I wasn't late, and the teacher thought my punctuality and breathlessness meant I was eager, which would explain why I always did my assignments perfectly. I wasn't eager. I was dying to get out of there but just couldn't conceive of what to do with the various exercise sheets we were given besides fill them in. Maybe it had something to do with being from Canada; the other kids didn't seem to feel that way. Some of the kids crumpled their sheets into balls and stuffed them in their desks, as if storing ammunition for a fake snowball fight. My brothers had warned me that there wasn't going to be much real snow. Winter would be greyer here, they said, because the sky wouldn't reflect the light from the ground.

P.S. 26 was an old brick building with bars on the windows like a prison. The walls inside were the colour of yellowing paper. The classrooms at my school in Chomedey had been large, clean and airy, with a lot of bright felt and plastic everywhere. During the school day at Crestview we would move to different rooms for math, French, social studies and gym. Some of these rooms had no walls or doors;

they were just wide-open spaces with low tables. The school certainly didn't look like a prison. But none of the other students, all of them white and Jewish, had ever called out personal observations in class. And until that day in the Bronx, I had never felt welcome. If I tried to speak to my classmates in Chomedey, or even pass something to them, like a crayon or a handout from the teacher, they would look at someone else and whisper that I was dirty and contaminated. The teacher would have never said *shut up*.

At lunchtime on that first day at P.S. 26, all the kids who weren't black walked out the door. There was a Chinese girl whose name sounded like Shy-Ann but who wrote it completely differently. Tsaioan was quiet and drew well. There were James and Kim, who stood out because of their milky-white skin. There was me. And there was Lois, who looked black but told me right away that she wasn't. "I'm Puerto Rican."

I wondered if that was why she got to go home for lunch.

"I'm Irish," said James. "My real name is James Patrick O'Donnelly the Second."

"Is your father a king?" I asked, wondering if his family was, like mine, in the wrong place.

"No, he's a cop."

"I'm Jewish," said Kim, and then, reading something on my face, "Hope that's okay." She had long reddish-brown hair and large brown eyes. Something about her reminded me of a dog.

"Where are the other kids eating lunch?" I asked.

"In the basement," said Kim. "They get welfare lunch. It's cool. They play Motown. Maybe they can invite you sometime when someone's absent."

In the afternoon, at the end of the school day, I walked home with the two kids who lived on my street. One of them was Kim, who lived in one of the brownstones. The other was Bradley, who lived right in our apartment building, on the same floor. He told me the building was supposed to be for people on welfare, and that my father must have been able to bribe someone to get us in. When I asked my father about it that evening, he said Bradley was smart but if he were smarter he would keep his mouth shut.

One Saturday morning, Kim, Bradley and I decided to meet at the park on the corner. It was a cool day; the sun was trying to break through the clouds. The park consisted of a fenced cement square full of broken swings and broken glass. There was a basketball hoop that was intact, but it was impossibly high and Bradley's ball leaked air. We sat on the broken swings and talked. Bradley had to leave after a while. He went to his aunt's place upstate on the weekends. As he was getting up from his swing, I asked him what upstate was.

"It's white. Where my aunty lives. Clean and white like a nice shiny toilet bowl."

"What is she doing there then?"

"She cleans toilet bowls, mostly."

When he'd gone, Kim told me that some of the kids thought Bradley was lucky, because upstate meant ponies and pastures. But Kim herself didn't agree.

"I love living in the city," she announced, as if she had lived somewhere else before.

"I wouldn't mind the city if it didn't smell so much," I said. "You know, in Chomedey we had real playgrounds. There were monkey bars, and slides, and—"

"No shit?" she interrupted, shocking me. She got off her swing, pushed me off mine, and ran out of the park, laughing. I got up off the ground and ran after her, and the next thing I knew, I was following her onto the subway to Manhattan.

The train was so old and noisy and shook so much that I was sure there was something wrong with it, and that we were going to die. I had been on the metro in Montreal, and it was smooth, new and quiet. There were lots of bad words painted on the walls on this train, *shit* and also ones that I didn't understand, only recognized. Kim looked unimpressed by everything, as if she were sitting in her living room, and it was normal to have a kind of earthquake every day. When the train jerked to a halt with a long screech I looked around and there was no reaction on any of the other passengers' faces. Everyone looked sleepy and sullen. Kim grabbed my hand and pulled me up off my seat and out the door.

We went to a theatre where you could watch three movies in a row, and where kids got in for free when accompanied by their parents. Kim lied and said our parents were already inside. The person taking the tickets raised her eyebrows disapprovingly.

"You must think I'm some kind of stupid nigga," she said, shaking her head, but she didn't stop us from going inside.

"What's a nigga?" I asked Kim as she chose our seats. There were only about ten other people there. The theatre was old and very ornate, with bronze statues and mosaic tiles, crystal chandeliers, a worn red carpet. The seats were padded and covered in red velvet. It was like sitting in a giant jewellery box.

"It's a negro."

"What's a negro?"

"It's a person," Kim said, looking around her. "Now shut up."

We watched one and a half Woody Allen movies but we were both very bored, and left in the middle of the second one.

"Sorry," Kim said. "I think my dad told me those movies were good."

"Tell your dad that kids don't—"

"I don't see my dad no more," she said, cutting me off.

On the ride back, Kim pretended to be me. She made shocked, frightened faces and even shrieked at one point when the brakes screeched. Some people looked up from their newspapers and asked her what her problem was. She just laughed and pointed to me. But she had this way of making fun of herself making fun of me.

"I know, I know. I'm hilarious. I should win an Oscar."

We stopped at her apartment, where someone who looked like a teenager was washing a little girl's hair in the sink.

"Alice and Tricia, my ma and my sister," Kim said carelessly, as we walked past them. Alice, Kim and Tricia looked like three versions of the same person, with the same long, reddish-brown hair. Alice was wearing a tie-dye t-shirt and cut-offs.

"You're so lucky," I said. "Your mother is so young. And you have a sister."

Kim opened the fridge door and peered inside.

"Get out of there!" Kim's mother snarled.

"Yeah, it's fantastic," Kim said dryly. "You must be so jealous. Let's go to your place."

My father was home. He was sitting cross-legged on the living room floor, his glasses on, reading the paper. I tried to introduce them to each other, but neither seemed interested. I went to the kitchen to fill a plate with cookies, and when I came back, Kim was walking around the living room touching things: a soapstone seal, a photograph of my mother holding one of my older brothers ages ago, a crystal candelabra. I put the cookies on the coffee table. She took two, and continued to walk around in circles around the table. My father finally looked up, and he and Kim began to have a conversation that I found hard to follow.

"Nice piano." Like the other kids at school, Kim had a way of talking that was polite and brazen at the same time.

"What does your father do?" my father asked.

"I dunno," Kim said. She was unfazed by his abrupt manner and his Indian accent.

"Where do you live?"

"Down the street. My parents are divorced or something."

"Or something?"

"Can I play?" Without waiting for an answer, she sat down at the piano and played something high and chirpy with her knuckles.

Kim left as my mother got home. My father spoke to my mother in their secret language. I waited while they argued and then came to an agreement, which they explained in English: I wasn't allowed at Kim's apartment anymore, although she could come over. I gathered that it was because Kim's parents were divorced. My mother said to make sure she didn't steal anything. Also, she said, Kim had to wash her hands first if she wanted to play the piano.

I thought about why I had never been able to make friends in Chomedey. Once in the second grade I made a friend, but he turned out to have something wrong with him. He was new there, and I told him his pictures of Super Hercules Man were great. He said, "My name is William," and, "Play with you at recess." I nodded, stunned. I worried about not knowing how to skip rope. I would have to tell him: the other kids let me be ever-ender sometimes, but I wasn't allowed to jump in. Would he expect me to know how? My stomach was in knots.

When the recess bell rang I watched him get up and leave the classroom. He didn't wait for me, and I figured I must have misheard him. But when I went outside, I spotted him alone, his small, scrawny body against the back wall of the school. As I skipped uncertainly toward William, I felt I could see my body skipping and it looked weird. A crowd of kids, flapping their fingers against their mouths and chanting, roared, "Wawawawawawawawas. A good Indian is a *dead* Indian. Wawawawawawawa." They went on like that for about half a minute. Then somebody found the skipping rope, so the roar got distracted.

"What was that?" William asked me.

I shrugged. He was new. He didn't know anything. He didn't have to know. I started to get stomach cramps, and pressed my thumbs in my sides to make them stop.

We watched the girls skip rope. A few boys jumped in too, but they weren't taking it seriously, just clowning around and making fart noises. I was relieved that they had enough kids, and wouldn't ask me to be ever-ender, because then they would probably have gotten William to sterilize the ends for talking to me. They would take him to the bathroom and run the hot water until it was scalding and make him scrub the plastic ends. That wouldn't have been the greatest thing to happen on your first day of school.

When recess ended and we went back inside, there were a few kids waiting by William's chair. As we approached, they pointed to a shape etched into the back and shouted that William was anti-Semitic.

"What? I am Jewish," William protested.

"What is that thing? Is it a Jewish thing?" I asked. It looked like something I had seen in a weird Indian painting we had at home, one that had given me nightmares. The painting showed an elephant with human hands and a fat man's breasts, elaborately bejewelled and dressed in yellow pants. A tattoo on one of its upturned palms. And the elephant's tattoo looked like this thing on William's chair, two pairs of legs joined in the middle, running in a circle.

"It's a Swastika. But I don't know where it came from," William said.

Anti-Semitic. Was that the opposite of antiseptic? I shuddered as I realized his chair was contaminated. I moved my books to a table at the opposite end of the room.

To my surprise, I did get invited to welfare lunch at P.S. 26. My mother insisted that I bring my own sandwiches anyway. The lunchroom was way down in the school basement, and as I walked down the first set of stairs, the words of a Jackson Five song wafted up the stairs. *Easy as one, two, three...*

By the time I had gone down the first set of stairs, I could hear kids clapping hands to the upbeat music. I felt like I had finally been invited to a party that I had wanted to go to for a long time but had never known about. All the kids were sitting on benches around a long row of tables. Dena sang out my name and made room on the bench for me. I walked across the room to her and sat down, feeling very self-conscious with my shiny Partridge Family lunchbox. The kids around me, ignoring their bowls of tomato soup, dancing in their little chairs to the Jackson Five, leaned in to look at it and said it was nice. I could tell they were laughing at it, but they did it in a friendly way, so it was like we were mocking my lunchbox together.

The kids around the table were wiggling and singing. *Simple as do re mi.* Bradley waved to me. He was holding an imaginary microphone and pretending to pass it around. When he extended his arm in my direction, I couldn't sing. I just froze.

"Okay. but next time I'm gonna get you, girl, you understand?"

Why couldn't I ever feel as comfortable as other people? Was there something wrong with my skin?

One Saturday I came home from playing with Kim and Bradley to find my parents arguing. It was a strange sort of argument: they kept repeating the same English sentences back to each other, as if they were taking an angry language class.

"I am not your servant, Baba."

"I am not *your* damn servant, Baba."

"You can clean the bathroom. I have other things to do."

"*You* can clean the bathroom. *I* have other things to do."

"Go to hell."

"*You* go to hell."

My father lunged toward my mother, his palm raised at the level of her face.

I ran between them, and screamed that it was okay, that I'd do it.

Both of them looked shocked. They hadn't noticed I was there. My mother didn't seem relieved that I had saved her. My father seemed to swallow something, maybe some bad words. At supper, both my parents looked guilty. They mumbled to each other in either Hindi or Punjabi and then they made an announcement in English. They agreed they would hire someone. She looked at my father and reminded him that they were saving a lot of money by living in a rent-controlled building.

127

In Chomedey, there had been fights that ended in hitting. One recurring one was about saving money. My father regularly drove miles out of his way to buy tomatoes on sale, and my mother would call him a *bev koof*. At school one day, I called William a *bev koof* when he tried to show me one of his drawings, but then told him to forget it when I realized that the words weren't in a language that he had ever heard. He looked at the picture I was drawing of a girl with long blonde hair, and mumbled that it was nice before returning to his seat.

Bradley stopped coming to school after a while. We heard that he went to live with his aunt after his mother got shot in the face by her boyfriend. I thought about how, if the boyfriend hadn't had the gun, he probably would have just slapped her. Kim told me that Bradley had asked her to go steady with him before he disappeared. I nodded solemnly, pretending to know what that meant.

One afternoon I came home to find Kim's mother in our bathroom. She was wearing the tie-dye t-shirt and cut-offs and was bent over the bathtub, scrubbing vigorously. Her long coppery hair was sprinkled with Comet. She looked up, saw my shocked face and gave me a quick grin and a wink. I couldn't make myself smile back. She wiped the sweat off of her face with her forearm and went back to work. I watched in amazement as she scrubbed the underside of our toilet seat.

"So Kim told me about Bradley," she said, shaking her head. "That poor boy. Moving to some white neighbourhood in the Catskills. How's he gonna survive there?" She mumbled something with swear words, something about wasps.

Marilyn Bombolé

My name is Marilyn Watson, but it used to be Marilyn Bombolé, and I'm thinking of changing it back.

I became Mrs. Watson two months ago, on a breezy blue August afternoon. We had a lovely wedding at a park near our home in Laval. It was marked by spontaneous bursts of beauty. My young cousins Miranda, Jacqueline and Audrey released a swirling orange cloud of butterflies as Greg and I were pronounced man and wife. His nephews, toddlers Louis and Ben, released soapy purple bubbles. My father made a humorous speech in his thick Cameroonian accent; until then I had thought of him as sweet, kind and earnest, but never funny. Greg's sisters Amanda and Monica broke into a song about how Greg and I had been each other's first crush.

This was almost true. I had been obsessed throughout high school with a boy called Michael Branigan. He used to play folk songs on his guitar, alone under a tree at the end of the schoolyard. His voice was soft and shy. He never knew how I felt, but I thought of him every day and every night. We never said much to each other, and I don't think he ever even smiled back at me. Later, when Michael dropped out of school, I found myself sitting next to a new boy who reminded me of him. That was Greg. He was only slightly less reserved. He didn't find it impossible to smile back.

I took Greg's name because I was tired of spelling mine over the phone. It was just another detail of matrimony that I hadn't given much thought to but was confident would end up working out. I have never applied for a job, as I am a dressmaker and I work from home. My clients come to me by word of mouth. But of course I know that with a name like Bombolé, had I ever applied for a job in writing I might not have gotten it. You could say that I decided on becoming a dressmaker as a preemptive measure, so that the racists would be sifted out before they got to my door.

Because I work from home and Greg is often on the road, I was the one who was responsible for finding a new apartment after we got married. I had been living in a studio in my parents' backyard, and Greg had been staying on extended visits, but it was time for us to leave. The first time I called about an apartment and left my new name on the voice mail, I was giddy with excitement and forgot to leave my phone number. When I called back, I remembered to leave my number but stumbled when leaving my name. When I finally managed to make an appointment I wasn't surprised when I was told, at the door, that the apartment had been taken: I was so mixed up.

However, this would become a pattern in the coming weeks. Several times, the eyes of the person at the door widened a little as the door opened a crack, and I was told the apartment had already been taken. There were exceptions, of course, but these apartments were sunless and smelled dank. Greg's only stipulations were that the apartment be bright and clean.

I told him on the phone one evening of my lack of success. His voice conveyed the disbelief of a decent white man who imagines the world to be a good, just place. He never actually said he didn't believe me, but when he asked me to keep trying, I didn't have the heart to tell him how much this was getting to me. I also thought, if he were black, he wouldn't even bother trying. Life is even harder for our men. I knew, growing up, from the strain and vulnerability in my father's eyes, that for a black man, it was hard to just exist. Maybe that is why I ended up falling in love with Michael, and then with Greg. They were loners and outsiders, but it was because they chose to be; there was a kind of strength there that I found attractive.

One day I answered an ad, as Marilyn Watson, for a large apartment near the river. The landlord told me his grandson would let me in to look at the place, and if I was still interested, I could fill out an application. It was mid-afternoon on a Sunday when I visited. A gorgeous, old Victorian building in a quiet cul-de-sac. Giant old oak trees, their thick leafy branches leaning towards each other in the middle of the street. I walked up the winding iron staircase and admired the traditional mouldings on the heavy oak door. I rang the doorbell, and as I waited, I felt increasingly excited. I thought, *this is the one*.

The person who answered the door had a bald head and piercing blue eyes. A face I recognized. And a tattoo I didn't, on his right arm. We stood blinking at each other.

"Michael Branigan," I said.

Back in high school, he'd had long, brown hair, while all the other boys were suede-heads. I'd loved him and his hair. He told me the apartment was taken, and his eyes told me he felt he owed me no explanation. He had the same soft voice, but there was no shyness in it. He stood above me in his grandfather's doorway, more muscular than he had been, more comfortable in his skin, more beautiful even as he peered down at me on the step. As I turned and walked down the steps, I wondered what had changed. I heard chattering above me and looked up to see three young men standing on the balcony. They wore white undershirts, the kind my father wore around the house. They beat their chests and made monkey noises.

After that day, I continued to look for an apartment but responded to the ads as Marilyn Bombolé. One person out of nine called me back, an old Haitian man whose first name was Parfait. He told me he had several apartments to rent out, and was sure one would be right for us. When I heard his name and his accent I told him my old name again, and found I enjoyed the sound of it.

Doppelgänger

I'm the kind of guy who is often mistaken for someone else. It has been happening to me since I can remember, but then, I'm the sort of person who doesn't remember a lot from before the end of high school. My girlfriend Tanya is pretty much the opposite that way, claims to remember everything from the first wrenching moment of her own birth. I think it has to do with the meaning she puts into events. Every moment is special, significant, original.

Strange then that Tanya's jealous of me and my everyman face. Maybe it's because she was an only child, a sort of afterthought, and she grew up lonely. Tanya's mother is Chinese-Canadian and her father is from Russia. You wouldn't think Tanya's mother was Chinese if you just spoke to her on the phone; she is something like third generation. But she grew up speaking Cantonese with her parents and later learned Mandarin at university. Her real love was the Russian language, though, which she ended up majoring in, and somehow everyone knew she would marry one of her professors. She married the oldest one. He was sixty-five when Tanya was born.

Before I met Tanya, I didn't know beautiful people could be lonely. She has a wide round face like the moon, sparkly deep-set blue eyes like a tiger, and a big red mouth with a little heart-shaped thing happening on the top of her upper lip. When we first met, she was studying music, and she dressed, like, unique, like she looked—these retro dresses, white boots, a furry little hat she called a pillbox. Later, though, she switched to dental hygiene. Now she just wants to look like everyone else.

When we were in university, we both worked at a record store on Mont-Royal called L'Échange. I always found it amusing how so many customers looking for a CD got the name of the band wrong. We got asked for everything from Earth, Wind & Water to the Bananarama Disco Club. They would mistake me for someone else too. At least once a week someone would stare at me while I was going about my duties as a cashier, punching in keys, slipping CDs in bags, and finally, when I turned and smiled, ask me if I was someone's brother, friend, old roommate or whatever. Tanya got jealous each time she witnessed one of these encounters.

I thought she was going to burst with excitement when one of our neighbours told her that she looked exactly like a model that she used to know. For Tanya, it wasn't so much the model thing that impressed her, as the idea that she had a twin out there somewhere. Of course, that her twin made money just looking at a camera did get her thinking as well: *I could be recognizable.* But then when our neighbour finally stopped Tanya in the hallway with a picture from a magazine, Tanya went silent with disappointment. The model, the supposed Tanya-double, was sitting in shadow. Her only identifiable traits were the brown hair, straight and long, and a pair of glasses. Tanya doesn't even wear glasses!

I guess the mix-ups started happening again last winter, when we were in Mexico. I went into a store to buy some sunscreen and noticed that the teenage girl at the cash was both smiling and trembling as she counted out my change. I smiled back and started to say a few clumsy words in Spanish, but she interrupted me to tell me she knew who I was.

"*Yo te conozco. De la telenovella.*" I know you. From the soap opera. She was so sure and happy. By the time I thought to ask her which telenovella, the lineup behind me had grown and she'd moved on to the next customer. When I told Tanya, she whined, "Why doesn't anyone ever tell *me* who I am?"

Things got weirder in May, just after we finished college and started our new careers. Way more people started staring at me. And all of these people looked sort of Chinese. One afternoon, we borrowed Tanya's mother's car and drove to Costco to stock up on cereals and canned tomatoes and stuff. Tanya drove in her competent but uncertain way. She doesn't drive very often and isn't used to it. She parked, and as we got out of the car, two slight figures with short black hair, a woman and her teenage son, got out of theirs. As soon as they saw us, they froze. They stood and stared at us.

"Did I park funny?" asked Tanya, frowning and examining her wheels and the lines around the parking space.

"No sweetie, you did fine." We were speaking to each other but kept glancing back at our observers as we crossed the parking lot and went into the Costco.

Inside the store, in the cereal aisle, it happened again. This time, it was a couple in their forties. Tanya was off in the feminine-hygiene section, so she didn't see them, but they gave me a startled look, looked at each other, and then stared back at me.

Then the following evening, my friend Steven and I went to watch the playoffs at a bar, Les 3 Brasseurs. The Habs were up one-nothing at the end of the first period when I ran upstairs to use the men's room. I heard a loud conversation in Chinese as I was climbing the stairs, and then when I reached the top of the stairs the talk suddenly wound down. There was a group of people sitting around a U-shaped table, and every one of them was staring up at me. Everyone except one guy at the far end who was engrossed in his food, but when the person next to him nudged him, he looked up at me, and the blasé expression on his face quickly changed to one of complete amazement.

In the men's room, I looked in the mirror as I washed my hands. At twenty-five, I could pass for twenty or thirty. Brown hair, glasses, slightly wide nose, pale face, thin red beard. Maybe a little thick around the waist. I could be anyone. But who was I to the Chinese?

On my way back downstairs I managed to stop their conversation again. They looked at me with something like happy surprise.

"Hello?" I heard myself saying, like someone answering a telephone.

"Hello," came the polite choral response.

"Uh... how are you guys tonight?"

There was a silence, and then a couple of them said, one chiming in a little late, "Fine, thank you. How are you?"

I smiled at them, but couldn't think of another thing in the world to say. Or rather, ask. What would the question be?

I went back downstairs. Steven and I talked about the hockey game, and about our new jobs, his as an accountant, and mine as a studio technician. We ordered another pitcher of beer. At one point, I thought of mentioning the people upstairs, and the people at Costco, but it wasn't the sort of thing that you tell Steven. After a while, I realized I had to go back to the men's room.

The Chinese conversation was very loud as I ran up the stairs. I considered continuing past their table, but as I arrived at the top step they abruptly stopped talking and looked in my direction. I gave them a smile and a half wave. Then, for some reason, I held up my finger in an international *wait a minute* and went into the men's room, where I looked at my face again. I had gotten new glasses recently, and Tanya said that the new lenses made my eyes look bigger. I washed my hands and examined my fingernails, which were neat and square. Nope, nothing to be learned from my fingernails. I thought of the Chinese people whispering about me, and decided to get to the bottom of it.

I strode out of the bathroom like an actor arriving on stage. The diners didn't clap, but they stopped whispering and looked up at me with expectant half-smiles.

"So how are you guys doing?" I asked again.

"Fine, thank you," they all said on top of one another.

"So… are you guys Chinese?" I heard myself say.

"Yes," they all chanted back.

I pulled up a chair from an empty table across the room and asked all of the other polite questions that came to mind.

"Are you tourists?"

"Yes!"

"How do you like Montreal?"

"Yes!"

"Well, that's good."

Someone shouted something in Chinese, and then there were several seconds of complete silence as they all stared at me shyly.

I tried French.

"Ça va?"

Only one person answered me, repeating the words back to me with the same intonation as in my question. He happened to be the one person wearing a shirt with English words written emphatically across the front. They said "You've gotta be kidding me."

There was another awkward pause, and then I got up and turned to go. They turned away and resumed their conversation and their beer drinking. As I began to walk away, a young man reached out and placed a hand on my arm and spoke to me quietly. I couldn't understand him, and I pointed to my ears. When he repeated himself I realized that he was speaking Chinese. I shrugged and smiled. He laughed, removed his hand and dismissed me with a wave. He had on the same shirt that Steven was wearing, a red and white checked thing that I had seen in a shop window on Ste. Catherine Street. I wondered if they had both gotten it there. Was shopping in Montreal worthwhile for a Chinese person? Was the shirt made in China? What was his opinion of globalization? There were so many things I wanted to ask but couldn't, because of the language barrier.

Everyone was drunk and having a good time. I didn't want to bother them anymore. I wondered if they had been making fun of me. It didn't seem that way. They seemed like a nice bunch of people. I started downstairs when someone else yelled something in Chinese. I turned around, but just got that friendly, expectant stare again.

The next morning, when I told Tanya the story, she responded by furiously washing dishes. She even took my cup of coffee, which was still pretty full, and plunged it, coffee and all, in the basin of soapy water, turning the suds brown and muddy. *Clank. Crash. Bang.* She was getting pretty rough with those dishes. Finally she looked at me and said, "Maybe you're like a Talento, one of those white guys in Japan who are famous for doing idiotic things." She wiped her hands on the top of her jeans. She set her mouth in an expression that seemed to say *I don't see why you get all the attention.* And then, as if nothing had just happened, as if everything was completely peachy between us, she said, "Let's go out to supper tonight. It's Saturday. A lot of couples go out to eat every Saturday night."

"No problem, Tan. Where do you want to go?"

"Chinatown."

"Right, of course." Neither of us smiled.

Tanya is allergic to MSG and knows I know, but I wasn't going to go there. We've been together two years now, and that still seems like a miracle to me. Tanya has got it all—brains, creativity, magnificent body and an incredible singing voice. I have a little garage band. It's just me, Steven, and another friend of ours. Tanya sometimes sings with us. I know she knows that fame for our band is not in the cards, and that a career in dental hygiene is a respectable choice, but when she sings she really gives it her all.

My life was a little messy before I met Tanya. Cigarette butts, empty bottles and the smell of bad breath, my bad breath, used to fill my apartment before she started to drop by. Now everything feels right.

Thanks to Tanya even my breath has improved and my teeth feel clean most of the time. Sometimes I lick the outer surface of my top teeth and enjoy that clean feeling and just feel lucky that Tanya is in my life. All this to say that I am the kind of guy who knows not to argue. I'd be risking way too much. So all I said about going to Chinatown was, "You know, I can't guarantee anything's going to happen."

The staring thing started on the 80 about six stops before we got there. A mother and her little boy both gave me The Look, and then when an old man got on he glanced at me, smiled knowingly, and then smiled in the same way at the mother across the aisle.

I looked at Tanya. Tanya looked pissed off.

A block into Chinatown she tapped my arm. We got up and rang the bell. As we got off the bus, I followed Tanya to a restaurant she knew, the Dragon Room. We turned quite a few heads. A teenage couple quickly snapped pictures of us on their mobile phones. Tanya opened a door and gave me a sarcastic "After you, sir" wave. We climbed a pleasantly greasy-smelling staircase. I wondered if anybody from the street would follow us upstairs, but apparently they believed in keeping a respectful distance. I found that admirable and thought of saying so to Tanya, but the set of her jaw kept me silent. The place looked less Dragon Room than Linoleum-on-Special; I wondered aloud which of the two would be harder for the Chinese to pronounce. Tanya didn't say anything. I'm such an idiot sometimes. A young man was sitting next to the "Please Wait to Be Seated" sign, apparently dozing. The walls were papered with panoramic pictures of an unidentifiable European city, all churches and canals.

A tiny woman with a hairstyle like a teacup appeared. She gave us the standard smile, which was suddenly replaced by a gaping sort of awe. She began speaking very fast in Chinese and had us follow her to a table. She went over to the guy who was asleep and shook him awake. They both began exclaiming over something. Then he came over to me and asked me something in Chinese.

138

I must've looked helpless in the face of everything they thought I could be. The woman, watching from the counter, laughed merrily and then came over and gave us a menu. She said something else in Chinese, and then Tanya said, "Uh, do you speak English or French?"

The woman's smile disappeared. She looked at me as if I would have something to say about this question. When I didn't say anything, she smiled at me anyway, as if we shared a secret.

"Okay, French. Français. Allez-y s'il vous plaît."

The restaurant gradually began to fill as we ate our dinner. People glanced at us and gave each other little taps on the forearm as they nodded in our direction and tried their best not to stare. Somehow, the more discreet they tried to be, the more scrutinized we felt. The food tasted wonderful, but I could tell Tanya was already starting to feel the MSG. She frowned as she ate, eating her noodles as if it were unpleasant work that she had to finish.

At the end of the meal, the formerly sleepy young man returned and asked me a question in Chinese. I said, "Pardon?" and he repeated, "Pardon?" and walked away laughing. He returned with a little brown teapot and a plate with two fortune cookies. I poured the tea as Tanya opened her cookie and read aloud: "If we do not change our direction we will likely end up where we are headed."

She grunted, raised her eyebrows and nodded at me to open mine.

"You will be the best," is what it said.

That was too much for Tanya. She actually said it; she said, "That was the last straw." She pushed back her chair and stood up and grabbed the bottom of her sweater and started to lift it over her bra. Before she could roll it over her head, though, I reached over and pulled it back down. A few people had gotten their cell phones out and were aiming them in our direction.

"Go ahead. Post your pictures on the Internet. My name is Tanya, by the way."

"Tanya, think of what your father would say."

"My father is an old man. He doesn't go on the net."

"Tanya, he'd find out. Tanya, we don't live in that kind of world where we can just do things anonymously."

We heard someone, somewhere in the restaurant, finally shout, "High five, Dashan!" The tables around us erupted in laughter, obviously at our expense.

Both of us thought the same thing. Tanya took her iPhone out of her handbag, her sweater now firmly back in place over her belly. She googled *famous white guy, China, Dashan*. In less than a minute she showed me a picture of a guy with my hair colour, my high forehead, and a pair of glasses not much like mine at all. Mine are large and round with dark frames; his were narrow, almost rectangular, with light frames. Also, he had a sharp pointy nose, thin lips, a long skinny neck. There was something decidedly birdlike about him. And he had no beard.

We both shrugged.

"He doesn't look like you."

"No, he doesn't."

"He really doesn't!" Tanya was clearly delighted. "Not to me anyway."

"Not to me either. But to other people, at least to some Chinese people, I am… "

"I guess you are Dashan."

"What does that mean?"

"Big mountain, apparently." Tanya said, reading aloud.

"So I'm fat?"

Tanya giggled now. She kept reading.

"So why is he famous?"

"He speaks Chinese."

"And?"

"That's it. He's this white Canadian guy who speaks Chinese."

"And?"

"Flawlessly. Apparently he speaks it flawlessly."

Tanya was smiling at me and it felt so good to see that again. She has got the most beautiful smile, these full red lips and perfectly white teeth. I suddenly remembered something that she told me strangers asked her every once in a while: *What are you?* If you saw her smiling you'd swear she was the most gorgeous woman in the whole world. I told her this, not for the first time, but for the first time in ages. She continued to beam at me, even as I added, in the best Russian accent I could muster, "But you know, if you go somewhere such as Mongolia, face like yours be dime for dozen."

"I think I'd like to learn Chinese," she said.

"Maybe we could take a course together."

Her smile grew even wider. "Let's go home and finish taking off that sweater," she said. She leaned over the table and kissed me, as the whole restaurant seemed to shake with the flash of cell phones.

The Dare

"How could you stand there in front of a bunch of strangers, stark naked?" Phil didn't get it, and that saddened Karen a bit. He usually got her perfectly.

"Well, for a shy person, it was the ideal job. I didn't have to talk to anybody, or make eye contact with anyone. It's like what I do now."

"Writing? How so?"

"I am a shy exhibitionist."

The first time Karen went outside naked was after that conversation, and it was because Phil had dared her to. He was curious about her past, about how much was still in her. In a way, her former life as an artist's model made it easier for her to take off her clothes. But the people she had posed for as they sketched were strangers, whereas the people who may or may not have been standing at their windows were her neighbours. Neighbours, she had learned, tended to judge.

When Karen first moved to Pierrefonds, she was friendly to everyone, and everyone was polite and icy towards her. She invited the women who lived next door over for coffee. The first one, a social worker named Denise, came but only stayed a few minutes. As Karen got up to walk her neighbour to the door, she looked at the untouched cup of coffee and plate of muffins and reflected that Denise was probably wary that she would become part of her caseload. Karen knew she must have appeared troubled, although she was only exhausted and overwhelmed from her move. As Denise went out the door, Karen timidly asked her if she could borrow her husband to help move a bed from one room to another.

"That is, if he doesn't have back problems," Karen added with a nervous laugh.

"Well, actually, he does," Denise said.

Karen apologized for asking, but half an hour later, Guy showed up at her door. Unsmiling, he asked her where the bed was. They went upstairs, moved it, and then he bolted out of the room as if pursued by wasps. He continued running down the stairs—Karen stood at the top of the stairs and called down, "Thanks, goodbye"— but there was no answer as he hurried out the door.

The other woman was Christine. She told Karen that she had intended to come over that day, but that both her husband and her father had bad colds. Karen didn't understand why that stopped her from going next door for a coffee, but she just thought, *that's all right, I gave it a try.*

About a year later, making small talk with Christine and her husband Robert, Karen mentioned that she didn't know how to program her thermostat. Robert's reply stunned her.

"Well, maybe you could get one of your men friends to help you."

Men friends? Was he referring to Karen's brother, the yoga classmates she occasionally carpooled with, her (gay) personal trainer? She hadn't met Phil yet. He wasn't in the picture back then, and after Robert's comment, she made sure to avoid dating locally.

Now, not wanting to disappoint Phil, holding his gaze, Karen took off her clothes and put them on a chair. They were in the living room. She took the three or four steps to the door, half-expecting him to call her back. He didn't, so Karen opened the door, went outside and stood on the front step for about two minutes. Not much happened. She wasn't cold. It was about seven on a Sunday evening at the end of July, a warm rainstorm brewing, pleasant enough. She felt breezes where we don't usually feel them: through her legs, on the tops of her breasts and on her nipples. She heard the sounds of cutlery clinking together, a faucet running and then being turned off, and an unseen woman calling her cat. Two cars passed by. In one, a child stared at her through the window and then turned and called to her parents in the front seat. That was all.

But Karen felt completely exhilarated.

She came inside, beaming.

"You look great!" Phil said.

"Thank you."

"Not just because you're naked."

"I know," she said, and they smiled at each other.

Later that evening, fully clothed, Phil and Karen went for a walk. As they left, it started to rain. They encountered the Morins, the family from across the street, arriving home from their own walk. The kids were Maélie, a dreamy, wild-haired redhead of about fourteen, and her slightly older, autistic brother Ludovic. The parents gave Phil and Karen a strange look, but then maybe that had something to do with the fact that it was raining. When it started to pour, Phil and Karen finally gave up. As they reversed direction, running home shrieking with laughter, they came upon Maélie standing still in front of her house, as the rain poured through her hair and clothes, soaking her.

Karen went outside naked again on Wednesday evening. She put the porch light on this time. It seemed to her that the street got a bit quieter, as if holding its breath. A teenage couple she didn't recognize passed. They were very deep in conversation, and didn't glance her way. But she felt watched nevertheless.

She did it again the following evening. This time she went down her front steps and stood in the moonlight. A few houses away, there were children playing on the street, which struck her as unusual. The children on this street were kept inside after supper, in front of screens. They did not react to her, though. It was if she and they were part of the natural landscape, like the birds in the trees. *I am at one with the universe*, she mused, smiling to herself. She did the Tree, a yogic position she had once tried to learn that required her to stand on one foot with the other tucked up inside the opposite thigh. For the first time, she had no trouble at all keeping the pose without wobbling. Her trunk was solid and straight, the sole of one bare foot rooted in the grass, the other curled up and nestled tightly inside the back of the opposite knee, her arms stretched out from her sides like strong branches.

On Saturday morning, Christine from next door beckoned to Karen as she was getting the newspaper from her front steps. Karen was apprehensive, but then Christine added, "My dad. He's painting eggs."

Painting eggs? But Easter was months ago. Since when did men, especially of that generation—Donald was ninety years old —engage in Easter egg design anyway? Christine put her finger to her lips as she led Karen through her house to the sunroom in the back, where her frail, bespectacled father was sitting across the room from a small table adorned with a red tablecloth and a small bowl of ordinary white eggs. Directly in front of Donald: an easel, a palette, an orange ceramic vase containing paintbrushes. His hands trembled slightly as he raised his paintbrush to apply a swirl of white paint to the canvas. He didn't hear them come in, absorbed as he was in his work. On the floor, against the wall beside him, were several other paintings. All depicted eggs.

Karen wondered why Christine had summoned her. It could be that like most people, Christine misunderstood what Karen did for a living, which was writing publicity brochures for art galleries. Maybe Christine thought her dad deserved some world renown in return for ninety years of dull existence. Or maybe Christine was

145

ready to move on to a deeper level of neighbourliness. Until now, they had never been in each other's houses, had never shared much besides shovels and tomatoes.

The fourth time Karen stood naked outside was the following Tuesday, later at night. She went down her front steps, crossed her yard and planted herself where the grass met the sidewalk, under a street lamp. The street was completely still, apart from the sound of crickets. She wondered if everyone was in bed, and then decided that she hoped so. When she had modelled for art classes, she had been young and unself-conscious. *No spring chicken anymore,* she thought, looking down at her stretched belly and dimpled thighs. *This will be the last time. I am running out of nerve here.* As she turned to go back into the house, she felt something bore into her right foot. Walking barefoot next to where the garbage got picked up probably wasn't the smartest thing to do. She lifted her foot, brushed her palm across the sole, and to her relief a piece of eggshell dropped onto the lawn. *Lucky. Maybe running out of luck, though.*

She came inside and found Phil waiting for her in the vestibule.

"It's okay," he said, studying her face and understanding everything. "You've been really brave."

He hugged her and told her that he had decided to take her advice and quit his job as a high school teacher and try to make a living singing.

"Brave and slave don't go together," he said simply.

"You make me happy when you sing," said Karen.

"You're not worried about money?"

"You could go to Vegas. I hear there's lots of money there."

"No, but seriously."

"You could be a singing teacher, Phil. You could teach the world to sing."

The next evening, as they returned from their walk, they heard a song they recognized from their university years. Then they saw

Janice, who lived next to the Morins, dancing on her front lawn in her nightgown. She had let her grey hair out of its bun and it swirled around her like a silver cape. Her lips were moving to the words of the song: *I would go out tonight/ but I haven't got a stitch to wear/ This man said/ it's gruesome/ that someone so handsome should care.*

On Sunday, Karen was pulling up dandelions from her front lawn with a weed whacker. A young blonde woman she didn't recognize walked by with a blond toddler and suddenly slowed her steps and called to her.

"Hey, what a great floppy sun hat!" the woman exclaimed.

Karen wondered if they had already met.

"Thank you… "

"What are you doing? Are you making holes in your lawn? Look Victor, she's making holes in her lawn. How curious!"

"I'm pulling out the dandelions."

"You're pulling out the dandelions?" She was obviously new to suburbia.

"Well, yeah," Karen said, secretly pleased that she didn't seem to get it, "I do it a bit for the neighbours."

"For the neighbours?!"

Karen decided she liked this young woman very much.

"Well, look, nobody else has dandelions." She indicated the immaculate lawns around her. "I don't think they like them."

"You could also just leave them… "

"Yeah, but sometimes you have to do things to get along with other people."

The young woman's name was Louisa, and she and Victor had just moved back in with her mother.

"I'm Janice's daughter. Do you know Janice?" Louisa pointed to their house.

"Oh, yeah, I know Janice," Karen said uncertainly; the truth was, she didn't *know* a lot about her until now. Until the dancing the other night, she certainly never would have pinned her as a Smiths fan.

147

"She's doing a lot better," Louisa said, leaning in conspiratorially.

"Oh," Karen said, raising her eyebrows and hoping her face was conveying sympathy and not complete confusion. Victor was pulling Louisa's hand and trying to drag her to the park, so Karen went back to work. Louisa looked back at Karen a few times as Victor pulled her down the street. Karen didn't let it show, but she was very pleased to have made a new friend. It was about time.

At night, Phil and Karen began to hear noises coming from one of the houses on their block. At first they thought it was cats in heat. Then they thought someone was in pain. Then, they wondered, *those* kinds of moans? From which house?

One morning Karen found a package of homemade cookies at her door with a note that said, "To my angel-hero, from the anonymous baker."

Then one day Christine invited Phil and Karen over for supper. *The first frigging invitation from anyone in ten years,* Karen thought. *I can't believe it.* They brought two bottles of white wine and half a watermelon. Christine's dad proudly introduced Tickle, their new beagle, and Tickle wagged his tail and happily piddled next to Karen's feet. Everyone laughed except Donald, who looked mortified and kept apologizing to her. They ate in the back yard. Phil and Karen noticed a change: the lawn was cheerfully overgrown. Christine served several courses of food: daikon salad, roasted carrots, zucchini in a tomato sauce, chicken breasts with lime sauce. Robert and Christine's son, Charles, an investment banker in his early thirties, arrived wearing bicycle shorts that Karen found tight, weird and hard to look at. As if sensing her discomfort but getting it all wrong, Charles looked deeply into her eyes all evening.

"Have you noticed that we've stopped mowing the lawn?" Robert said happily, his eyes sparkling. His hair, white with a few streaks of black, seemed longer too.

"That's such a good idea, Robert," Karen said, thinking of their new neighbour, Louisa. " Let's make it a movement. Enough with the mowing and weeding. I wonder if we could get Denise and Guy to join us."

"Oh, I think it's just Denise now," said Christine. "Guy's gone. He's left her. He was obsessed with some other woman."

"Oh, that's really sad," Karen said, surprised.

"I know. Poor Denise. She didn't know what was wrong and then he finally told her. He'd just stand and stare out the window all the time until she asked him, and then he finally told her."

Karen nearly choked on her wine. Phil stroked her arm reassuringly.

"Told her what?"

"What do you mean? He told her what was bugging him, that he was obsessed with some woman."

"Oh."

The four men—Phil, Robert, Donald and even Charles— exchanged looks.

A pause. Then, chimes. They heard the knife-sharpening man's truck roll slowly into the street.

A few evenings later, Karen was sitting alone at her picnic table in the backyard, listening to the crickets, when Denise suddenly appeared through the crack in the fence that separated their properties. She was walking slightly unsteadily and holding a glass of red wine. She sat down across from Karen and gave her a rather frightening smile.

"Good party the other night?" she asked, and then cackled. "Were they talking about me?"

Although ten years had gone by since Karen had tried to befriend her next-door neighbour, they had never stood on each other's property, nor discussed anything much besides the weather, what exactly they were supposed to put in the recycling bin, how much the tinker charged, and for what sized blade. Once Denise and Guy had tried to get Karen and Phil to share the cost of setting a skunk trap, and Karen had told them that she *liked* skunks. Karen was silent now, trying to think of an answer, as if trying to figure out how to say something in a foreign language.

"Are you afraid of me? Are you afraid of Virginia Woolf?" Denise asked, and cackled again. Then she grew quiet, but her smile stayed.

"That's funny. I used to be afraid of you," Denise continued after a while.

"It wasn't my… it wasn't what I did that… "

"What?" Denise shouted.

"I didn't think… with my clothes off, you know, I'm not young anymore, and I'm not exactly voluptuous…"

"Yes, yes, quite true," Denise said impatiently. "Anyway, it's much better now that he's gone. Good riddance to her too."

Her. Karen felt both relieved and bewildered. Denise had jerked her chin toward a house across the street and to the left.

"The boys have grown up and left," Denise went on, "so what did I need him for? To move my bed? Not likely!"

Denise laughed again. Karen wondered if she could be excused.

"You know," Denise continued, "when you are in a shitty mood and you just need a guy whose shoulder you can cry on?"

Her voice was getting softer and friendlier now. Karen nodded and smiled sympathetically.

"Well," Denise said, abruptly pushing herself up from the bench and shouting again. "He was NEVER that guy."

"To hell with him, then," Karen said, imitating Denise's drunken voice, but she immediately regretted her lack of inhibition.

Denise didn't notice. She just said, "Exactly," and waved her glass at Karen before turning toward the gap in the fence. She added, shouting over her shoulder, "Mid-life crisis. What a cliché."

Going off with that young blonde and her little boy. Karen despised clichés. They kept getting in the way of her writing, like weeds.

"And that stupid old cow, with her stupid records and her

stupid nightgown," Denise shouted out her kitchen window.

The words took a moment to digest.

As Karen returned inside the house through the back she saw Phil ahead of her down the corridor, closing the front door. In his hands: another bag of baked goods. They smelled wonderfully nutty.

The Holder

Matt was whispering something in Evie's ear as she slept. She woke up and he was hovering over her, expecting a reply. His hair and eyes were wild.

"What did you say?"

"Remember we said that all those people who called us losers when we were in high school are the losers now, and all of us, the ones who were the losers back then, are, like, hip?"

He spoke very fast and it took her a few sleepy seconds to digest his words. She wasn't used to hearing him like this. Only waking up in the morning did he speak so quickly, and without a single swear word interrupting his thoughts.

"Yeah, that's right, baby," she said slowly, after a while.

"Yeah," he said, much louder now, "but those people, the ones who called us losers, they're the ones ruling the world now!"

She hushed him, kissed his woolly hair, hugged him and patted his back.

But in her heart, she knew that he was right and vaguely realized that she had been dreaming the same thing.

Evie had overheard a conversation on the train the day before. One middle-aged woman approached another, shouted, "Katie!" and the other exclaimed, "Donna!" After a moment of reminiscing and comparing marital and reproductive history, Donna said,

"Wow, did you ever guess that Stephen Harper would be prime minister someday?" and Katie said, "Well, I think someone, in fact, wrote that on his yearbook page, but actually, I don't remember him. I was only there for half of Grade 11; I hardly knew anyone."

What she didn't say: *I was a loser. My parents were hoping things would work out for me at that school, but it was the same as always. I stuttered, I had pimples, I was grotesquely overweight, I had bad eyesight but felt that wearing glasses would be the final straw, so I was always bumping into things, to the general hilarity of the staff and student body. I think I had a nickname, although not the kind people say to your face. I think it was Bump.*

Evie knew all the words.

Evie and Matt had known each other since high school. Evie was the nearsighted lumpy one, and Matt was clumsy and had Tourette's. Both had been adopted; Matt had a brother who could pass for a blood relative but who was self-confident in a way Matt could never be. Evie didn't have any siblings, and she kept to herself, rarely making an effort to make friends.

The thing about being adopted was that although your parents were always saying that you had been chosen, unlike other children, who just came along, you knew that someone had also chosen to abandon you. And if it had happened once, your subconscious knew and occasionally whispered to your heart, it was bound to happen again.

When Evie and Matt met, it was like recognizing their other halves. They had carefully avoided each other, making excuses when they were assigned to work on group projects together, sitting as far away as possible from one another on the bus home, and only started their relationship twelve years later, when they met in a line at an unemployment office.

Before they met again, Evie had had a series of lovers she tried to turn into boyfriends. Matt had just come out of a ten-year relationship with a woman who was raised not to say "please" or "thank you." and who had never treated him very well. When Evie asked him why he had stayed with her, he told her he never thought he could do better than a 4. He never thought anybody above a 4 could love him. But this woman, she was a 5, so that was something. Matt refused to give Evie her rating, but she was pretty sure she was at least a 6, now that she had slimmed down a bit.

Evie and Matt were looking for an idea to become millionaires as quickly as possible. They were living in a shack in the woods. It had plastic sheets instead of windowpanes, and duct tape holding everything up. The reason for the duct tape was that they didn't have any money for tools, but they had found a roll of the stuff in a plastic bag behind the house. They often mused about all of the more useful things they could have found: a hammer, a screwdriver, a kettle, a whole chicken, a suitcase full of hundred-dollar bills.

Evie told Matt that before their rediscovery of each other she dated a Russian she had met on the Internet. Vadim had been obsessed with making a million dollars by inventing something that he could sell for a dollar apiece. Evie told Matt now that she'd had an idea at the time, but selfishly kept it for herself, in case she ever found herself troubled by a similar obsession. Which was very wise of her, she felt, in hindsight. At the time she'd had a secure job as an elementary-school teacher, but was forced to leave in disgrace when, because of a misunderstanding, the Russian uploaded nude pictures of her onto her Moodle page, the web page where she posted homework assignments. Vadim had left her sleeping, skipped across the room to the computer, where she had been working before their late-afternoon lovemaking, and, believing he was doing a very funny and delightful thing, transferred pictures of her, unmistakable curly auburn locks running like a trestle along each side of her naked torso. The misunderstanding was apparently due less to the fact that he understood very little English than because he had very little common sense. She promptly banished Vadim from her life, but from time to time did think of the Idea.

"Fucked. What is it? Shit."

They squeezed each other. They were in bed with only one thin, worn, green blanket and each other for warmth. Through the plastic sheeting: cold, wet gusts.

"A holder."

He held her and waited quietly, ear against her cheek, listening for the rest. She didn't say anything else, though.

"Prick. To hold what?"

Evie laughed at that. *Usually he doesn't mind if I laugh. But only me.*

"Shopping lists."

"Chicken," said Matt. "Fuck. Prick. Fuck you. Like on a wall? I think they have those."

"Yeah, but they are useless. You don't take your wall with you when you go to the grocery store. You need a *holder* for a list. On the cart."

"Grocery. Chicken. Shit. Prick." Matt said wistfully. He made a gurgling sound, like water going down a drain. He took a deep breath.

"What's bothering you, sweetie?" Evie knew that the Tourette's typically made its appearance before Matt was even aware of something bugging him. It never stayed that long at a time either. It was like a boy messenger that ran onto a stage, shouted something and then disappeared again.

"Dunno. Hungry, I guess."

The sun was just coming up. They hadn't eaten much except for Skittles and toast for a couple of days now. Bringing up lists on grocery carts, Evie thought, was probably a bad idea.

"I'll ask Pat what he thinks," Matt said, stunning her.

Pat was Matt's brother. He was a patent lawyer. He had been two years ahead of them in high school, a football hero, popular with the girls, but Evie had never met him. She had seen him on TV, on a high school quiz show. He had seemed to know an awful lot

155

about the economy for a teenage boy. Matt had always said that Pat was an asshole, like their dad. Their father had been a womanizer and a fraud artist. He was Pat's real father, as far as Matt knew. Evie thought it sucked, that both Matt's biological father and his real father had been of no help in terms of providing him with a decent role model.

Matt got up then, and actually started getting dressed. Evie asked him where he was going.

Deep breath.

"I'll ask Pat if it's a good idea or not. He'll know. He sees dozens of ideas a week."

"You're going over to Pat's?"

Matt, hopping on one foot, pulled a leg through his black denim pants, paused and looked at her.

"No, I'd better go to his office. Prick. I'm pretty sure it's a week-day today."

"Chances are, I guess," Evie said.

"Wanna come with?"

"Sure," Evie said. "It's not every day that I get to meet a rich asshole." She daydreamed, for a minute, about knocking Pat off his swivel chair and stealing his wallet, like a superhero for the honest poor.

Most people would call first, but Matt couldn't talk on the phone, and Pat had never met Evie. What would she have said? What would he have answered? She put on a long-sleeved dress from her teacher days and pinned her hair up. Then she reached for Matt's hand and they walked out of their shack, through the woods to the highway, and along the shoulder, occasionally stopping to put their thumbs out. Nobody stopped.

"I think we look too happy," Evie said.

They walked the four kilometres to the city outskirts and took the commuter train. It was crowded, as usual, with mildly unhappy people. Everyone was going to work. Resigned, silent, sleepy people of all ages and kinds. A young woman wearing green eye shadow and a hijab met Matt's eyes and then looked away. *He's so good-looking*, thought Evie, *I wish he knew*. A teenage boy nodded to the rap music coming out of his earphones and occasionally yawned. The plump white-haired woman next to Evie also nodded, absently but on beat.

A thin man with skin so dark it shone like polished wood seemed to be trying to catch a few more minutes of sleep, and frowned, though he kept his eyes closed, every time the intercom robot lady announced a stop. *I could get a job*, thought Evie gloomily. *Any old job. I guess it's my responsibility.*

Evie and Matt emerged from the station and crossed the street. They stood in a park holding hands and watched the ducks in a pond for a few minutes. Then they reluctantly went back across the street again, walked around the corner and entered an office tower. They took the elevator up four floors to Shultz and Hudon.

The receptionist was exceptionally pretty, with the kind of beauty, thought Evie, that *made you wince*: blonde ponytail, blue eyes, button nose, Barbie body. She greeted them as if she had been waiting for them all morning. She looked *so* excited. Despite being of a decent height, she seemed small. The ceiling was very high, the reception area very empty, except for her wide beige desk against a wood panelled wall. Evie wondered why such a classically beautiful woman, with all the choices in the world, would choose to work here. She wondered how much money she made, and whether it would be worth it to give up permanent unemployment to sit at a desk waiting for people all day.

"Hi, is Pat the patent lawyer in?" asked Matt rather smoothly.

The receptionist's face fell for the briefest moment, as if she was suddenly reminded that nobody ever came to see *her*. Then her smile came back, brave and dazzling.

"Who wants to know?" she asked in a joking voice.

"I'm Matt, the brother."

"You're Matt? I'm Matilda." She went on to say that Pat and his family were away on a camping trip that week, as well as the next.

"Shit," said Matt.

Evie's heart sank for everybody. But it could have been so much worse, she thought. *Lots of people say "shit."*

Matilda's smile didn't completely go away, but sort of changed shape, became slightly more oval. The telephone rang.

"Next time," she said helpfully before answering the phone, "you might want to call first." She pushed a business card toward the edge of the desk.

Matt took the card, glanced at it, but didn't move. He stared at Matilda.

"Bye, Matilda," Evie said, waving to her as she grabbed Matt's hand and pulled.

They took the train back. Evie circled the name and phone number of a temping agency advertised in the free paper. They walked home hand in hand.

"So… I could get a job. Or… we could write Pat a letter," Evie said. "Do people still do that?"

"We shouldn't have sold our computers," Matt said. "This is no way to live. Prick. Fuck."

Evie looked around for some paper, but only found some yellow Post-Its that she had grabbed as she left her classroom that last day. Then she remembered something, something good to say.

"You know, you were pretty good in that office today," she said, taking Matt's hand and pulling him onto the bed with her.

They lay in each other's arms quietly.

"She wasn't too bad either," Matt said after a moment.

Evie didn't ask him what he meant.

The temp agency seemed to like Evie's vagueness about her job history, and immediately offered her work when she called. For the next few weeks Evie worked at a bra factory in the old warehouse district, not as a receptionist, but for a surprisingly decent wage nonetheless.

Her days consisted of sitting in a dusty room surrounded by busty mannequins, helping her elderly boss fill out various forms. Sometimes Evie's workdays seemed endless, but she kept reminding herself that money was finally coming in. Every evening, when she came home, she half-expected to find Matt silent and drawn, with resentment or worse, depression. Instead, with that sweet smile of his, he told her he appreciated her more, and he appreciated the groceries too, as he took her bags from her and began making supper. All this food looked good on him. Although Matt was the kind of guy who did pale and skinny very well, the new healthy bloom on his face didn't do him any harm.

Evie made enquiries about work for Matt. Work that didn't involve talking to anyone. Yes, he could use a computer. But interviews, she knew, were impossible for him. When she got her second paycheque, she bought him some new clothes as he had requested. New jeans and boxers. He undressed and she pretended to try to stop him from putting on his new clothes. She crawled on him, tried to climb him like a tree as he tried to change.

"Hey, why are you pulling me off of you?"

"Silly. Do you want me to change or not?"

"No. Don't change. I like your naked skin. You smell nice for a bum."

"Thank you. Do I smell like a bum?"

She sniffed his stomach.

"No, you smell a little perfumey."

Matt's whole body stiffened. He clasped both of her wrists, extended his arms straight in front of him and pushed her away.

"I didn't realize Mister Matt was so defensive of his masculinity," she teased. "I didn't say you smelled like a woman."

Matt looked alarmed. He mumbled something about washing himself with shampoo. Then, "Matt. Don't tell. Fuck."

"What?"

"Nothing. Fuck."

"So I'll buy soap," said Evie, although frequent showering wasn't usually Matt's thing. He hated coming out of the shower. He was very sensitive to the cold. Evie's skin was too sensitive for soap, so she never bought any for herself. And although she had told Matt he smelled nice, the scent of his stomach was tickling her nose. She was allergic to perfume.

The next evening, walking home through the woods, Evie realized she was in pain, and stopped to remove a stone from her shoe. She held onto the thin trunk of a sapling to balance herself as she lifted her right leg, put a finger in the back of her shoe and peeled it off. A branch of the sapling snapped against Evie's weight. Suddenly, a bush next to her shook and a fox sprang out and flew down the path. Evie laughed. "You're beautiful!'" she called out after it. She couldn't follow it for very long; it disappeared quickly from Evie's field of vision. She needed new glasses. Not having a medical insurance plan really sucked. Oh, but its perfect stealth, its gorgeous haunted eyes, its thick coat, bright as a flame. She wouldn't forget any of that. She wished Matt had been there to witness it.

She heard some soft squeaks. More perfect beauty? She pushed the bush slightly and peered through the branches. What she saw made her step back in disgust: a mole, lifeless and staring, its mouth covered in blood, another bloody hole in its abdomen, being eaten by a small circle of tiny fox cubs.

A breeze like icy breath blew against her neck. November now. They'd had plans to winterize the shack, but it wasn't going to happen. Evie didn't know how she knew. She just knew. She imagined a wolf blowing the shack down.

When she got home, Matt was waiting for her with the news that Pat had invited them out to dinner, but that she didn't have to come.

"Tonight? How did this come about? Hey, I'm really worn out. I just got home." She decided she was too tired to tell him about the foxes. "I'm going in the shower."

Their shower consisted of a mounted hose behind a plastic curtain in the corner of the kitchen. They had to stand in a children's wading pool, instead of a tub. After Evie finished her shower, she slipped in a small puddle of water next to the pool and almost tripped over a floor heater that seemed to have appeared out of nowhere.

"Where did this come from?"

"I bought it this morning. Fuck."

"Are you trying to kill me?"

No answer.

"You went out this morning?"

"Yup. Ran into. Motherfuck. Fuck. Went to see. Prick. Pat."

"Oh really?" Evie was surprised. "That's great."

"We'll see."

"Okay."

Evie decided she might as well come along for the ride.

They met Pat at a French restaurant not far from Shultz and Hudon. Pat was taller and broader than Matt, but their features were very similar. He was more self-confident than Matt, but then, Evie reflected, most people were. Although lately, Matt really hadn't been too bad. For a guy supported by his girlfriend, unable to work because of a debilitating nervous affliction, he seemed okay these days.

"It is a pleasure to meet you, Evie," said Pat.

"Same here," Evie said. "Matt has told me so much about you."

"The lamb is good here," Pat began to say.

"I could never eat lamb," Evie said, and put her hand on Matt's arm.

"Me neither, actually. Nor veal. Like eating babies," Pat agreed.

"But you must try the French onion soup," he continued. He looked at Matt. "Matt, you are going to love this soup."

The evening went on like that, vague niceties gently tossed back and forth across the table like a ping-pong ball. Waiting for the soup, which Pat kept raving about. Finally, Evie put her arm around Matt and asked his brother if he had heard about how they were thinking of applying for a patent.

"Oh, is that what he was up to?" Pat said, as the brothers raised their eyebrows at each other. "I thought it was something else."

Evie was puzzled by this.

"Well, it's, it's kind of a stupid idea, Evie," Matt said, shocking her.

"A stupid idea?" Evie repeated sharply.

"Well, you know, it's like the thing with the Crocs. It could work for awhile, but then nobody would need them anymore."

Crocs were indestructible. That was the trouble with Crocs, Evie remembered.

"You know, maybe we would get some orders from some supermarkets, and then, nobody would want anymore, and then we would still have to pay for the infrastructure and the staff and… "

"Oh, is this the thing Matilda was talking about, the holders?" Pat interjected. "I suppose the Velcro might peel off at some point. Still… this *is* the idea with the supermarket carts, right?"

Evie heard Matt's full sentences echoing in her ear, and Pat's questions, and wasn't sure how to process any of it.

"Yeah, but it's a stupid idea, right?" Matt said.

"Yeah, pretty stupid," Pat answered, and the brothers laughed.

Evie frowned. She tasted her French onion soup. It was *awful*.

"So what is this meeting about?"

Pat cleared his throat and shot Matt a look across the table.

"Nothing," Pat said. Both brothers laughed a little.

"I thought Matt should try this soup," he continued after the uneasy laughter and the silence. "I want to see if it triggers something, something like recognition. I know it did for me."

Evie gave Pat a puzzled look.

"It's good, isn't it?" Pat asked Evie politely. He was smirking.

"Why don't *you* try it?" Evie muttered, expressing her anger in the only way available to her. Gruyere cheese had never been her favourite. *It tastes like…*

"Yes, good idea, I will." Pat took a sip of the soup, sat back, and motioned to Matt to do the same.

It has an odour, thought Evie. *It invades your senses. It smells and tastes like…*

Pat looked at Matt and waited until he looked back at him with childlike surprise.

A woman, thought Evie.

"Matilda," Matt said, and then he said, "fuck cunt."

"I know, right?" Pat said, over and over on top of what Matt kept repeating. "It tastes just like Matilda."

"Sorry," Matt said sheepishly to Evie, as if it were nothing. And then, "I *told* you he was an asshole."

Evie pushed her chair back and stood up. The background music suddenly seemed loud. It was *valse musette.* She left the restaurant without a word.

In the taxi, Evie hectored the driver to hurry up, worried that the brothers would have time to catch up to her. The window was open a crack and the air smelled white, like winter. She wondered if the baby foxes were still around. The accordion music from the restaurant continued to resonate in her head. She wondered if it was the money in her pocket that made her feel ruthless and free.

Elephant Heart

An old man, a complete stranger, recently asked me if I wanted to know the secret to life. I was walking down a street in my town, a leafy, moderately if unevenly well-heeled suburb, the kind of place you'd expect to find women over thirty-five doing yoga on fresh spring mornings. This guy was about seventy, in what must once have been a dapper blue pinstripe suit. I didn't see him coming when he suddenly approached and offered me his burning secret.

That man was brave. Maybe we both were. My town was the sort of place where people didn't really talk to each other, where you might know your two next-door neighbours, but that was about it. It was a problem in society as a whole, I knew, one that was regularly discussed in the media. Everyone complained about it, about this needless suspicion of one another. But you had to start somewhere.

What was the secret to life?

"It's to take every possible moment and milk out the joy, just spread the happiness everywhere," according to the man in the pin-stripe suit.

"I completely agree," I had told him. Who could argue with that?

Ben and I were lucky. We had found each other at work. Both of us divorced, me for many years and with two teenagers. We all got along well, though my kids could be sulky. You never knew what they were thinking, but then, adolescence was that sort of period. A difficult transition.

We found the armchairs on the Internet. We decided to get rid of my old loveseat and an end table that had belonged to Ben's previous apartment. We simply put them outside with our garbage, and the next day they were gone. Then we decided to buy the two maroon leather armchairs. They looked good in the picture, and they were cheap.

When we got to the house, we found a sad man in his forties and a couple of obliviously joyful little girls. There was a bowl of potato chips on the coffee table, and broken chips on the Oriental rug, which was worn and damaged but must have been beautiful at some point.

"My marriage is breaking up," the man told us. "I am moving into a small apartment. These chairs are really good, and not even a year old. They're recliners, you know. They go back like La-Z-Boys. You're getting a good deal."

"You're taking both?" one of the girls wailed to us, though she was making a happy, goofy face. "AAAWWWWW."

Her sister chimed in for a while. The girls each sat in a chair, swinging their legs. They were very small and thin. Their hair, a mousy shade of brown, was very greasy, and their skin was an unhealthy grey. But they laughed and shrieked as they leaned back and the chairs leaned back too. Their father didn't seem to notice.

When we had finished stuffing the chairs into the U-Haul and were about to leave, the man came up to the window carrying a giant stuffed toy elephant.

"You know anyone with little kids," the man stated, rather than asked. "Maybe they'd like to have this."

We couldn't say no. The man just looked so desperate. When we got home, we filled our living room with two new maroon leather recliners and one grey elephant. The elephant was torn in the bum, and very heavy for a stuffed toy. When we examined it we found it contained a broken gizmo that must have once made it talk; that was what accounted for the weight.

When my kids came home from school they both threw their bags on the floor and asked us what an elephant was doing in the room. I told them the story. Neither said anything. Everyone liked the chairs, but somehow we didn't use the living room as much as we had before.

One sunny day Ben and I were going for a stroll in our neighbourhood. I happened to look into an upstairs bedroom window of a house with green shutters. There was a small child's, perhaps a baby's, bedroom, decorated in pastel colours. In the window, there was a female version of our elephant. Female, because it had long spindly eyelashes and a pink bow next to each ear.

Ben reached for my hand, laced his warm fingers in mine, and asked me what I was thinking about. I had been thinking about a house I had lived in with my kids and their father, when the kids were very little. Their bedrooms had been painted blue with white clouds on the ceiling. But what I told Ben was that I was very happy, that it was a beautiful day, and that I couldn't believe my luck. I squeezed his hand.

On Valentine's Day, I took the day off to make a special meal for Ben. I grabbed my reusable shopping bags, put on my winter jacket, my knitted cap with the flaps and my boots and headed toward town to shop for the meal. I carried the elephant, a tiny envelope pinned to his chest. Inside the envelope was a small glass heart I had found in the basement amongst my daughter's abandoned craft kits, and a note:

To my beautiful elephantesse,
I saw you through the window. Here is my heart. Please accept it.
I put the elephant on the front porch of the house with the green

shutters and continued into town. I bought a bottle of wine, a steak, some tomatoes, mushrooms and artichokes. On the way home, I walked by the house again. The elephant had been brought inside. I smiled to myself. I glanced up into the bedroom but couldn't see inside; there were light curtains now that obscured the view.

And downstairs, I suddenly realized, a woman was staring at me through the living room window. She was blonde and wore red lipstick. She looked a bit like Drew Barrymore. She also looked completely terrified.

A Bear, Alone

My brother Jonathon's love life is a mess. He left his wife for a young German fan last year but, after several months of a long-distance relationship, she decided to "disembark from the dream," as she put it. Meanwhile, his children won't talk to him and every time he tries to talk to his wife, she says things that make him want to kill himself.

Only a handful of people showed up to this gig, a little one in Northern Ontario at a barn-turned-concert hall. It was drizzling and cold. The applause was polite. It had taken us five hours to drive there, and three and a half hours for the band to set up. After the show, every time Jonathon checked his cell phone or disappeared to the bathroom, I held my breath.

I was accompanying my favourite band, the Four Wheels, which happens to feature both my boyfriend Eli, on bass guitar, and Jonathon, on drums. Every time I am asked if I am part of the band I have to explain that I just go to the shows and sell the CDs. They don't trust me with anything else, although I bet I could bring in a lot more people if they let me sing. There are two other Wheels, a guitarist called Jill, who everyone expects to sing, probably because she is a woman, but who insists on just playing the guitar with the kind of grim concentration that makes her seem almost autistic; and her brother, the actual singer and head honcho, who we call

Honcho. His real name is Marvin, but he hates it because in high school everyone thought he was gay, since he both painted and played the piano, so his name was a source of torment. I love the name Marvin and I love Marvin Gaye, but I guess he finds Honcho more macho or something. I think he should get over the gay thing, but the boys won't let me go there.

Honcho and Jill got a lift back to the city with the soundman after the gig; Honcho has a new daughter and is completely in love. He was going to get home at four in the morning, but his wife Janey would likely not mind; she would probably be sitting in an armchair in a soft pink nightgown with a blanket over her, nursing little Melinda. Honcho could make Janey a cup of tea and he could sit close to her, maybe on the arm of the chair, and watch their daughter's eyelids flutter as she sleepily drank. I think love is the most gorgeous thing; it makes up for the rest, like badly attended, remote gigs and horrible hours, but it's not something I can talk about when Jonathon is around these days.

Eli, Jonathon and I had already accepted the offer from the concert promoters, Mitch and Lisa, to stay in their home, a tall, classy, immaculate modern cabin in the woods, with floor-to-ceiling windows. They had us follow them there in our car, and then they drove off and went to sleep at somebody else's house. They said they did that every weekend, that they got offers from people in the area to go crash at their places so that they could let the visiting musicians stay at their house. I think it is fishy; I think they are swingers or something. I don't understand why couples feel they need other people. Eli and I fit together in a way there is no room for anybody else. We toned it down a bit out of respect for Jonathon, untangled ourselves from each other when we felt him approaching. But anyway, the cabin was lovely. Jonathon didn't want to sleep. He wanted to drink like a rock star, so we shared a bottle of gin and stayed up half the night playing darts in one of the basement bedrooms. At one point I was too drunk to stand up, so I got under the covers

169

in the bed, sat up and threw my darts from there. Eli didn't drink that much. I could feel him watching us, as if trying to understand where we came from.

In the morning, I woke up with a headache. Eli massaged my temples in the unfamiliar bed, but it was Jonathon's hangover that I was worried about. We got up and listened for sounds from his room. The floor was cold, but we were cozy in the matching blue and white knitted socks Eli's mother had given us for Christmas. After awhile, I went to check on Jonathon and bring him a pair of slippers I found by the front door. I stood outside his bedroom and sang out softly, the way I used to when we were little—

"Are you sleeping, are you sleeping, brother…" I was answered by a loud sigh.

I opened the door a crack. Jonathon was sitting sideways on the bed, back to me, staring out the window. I stood there, hurting for him. I wish I had thought of slapping him when he first got involved with that Eva chick. What else are sisters for?

"I'm coming," he said finally, although he showed no sign of getting off the bed.

"Do you want to wear these slippers? The floor is cold."

"They don't fit."

I just stood there until he turned around.

"Maybe they fit Eli," he said. "They're way too tight on me."

I went to the kitchen and made some coffee. Eli and I waited for Jonathon at the kitchen table. After a few minutes, he came in, nodded to us, frowned, placed his hands heavily on the table and lowered himself into a chair. Then he gazed down, his long, wavy bangs covering half his face, and seemed to study both his hands and the black and white pattern of the tablecloth.

"Headache?" asked Eli, and pushed the coffeepot and a cup towards him.

"No, I'm all right."

Heartache, I thought. I wanted to hug him.

"There's no milk, cream or sugar," Eli warned.

"Figures. Maple syrup will do," Jonathon said, spying some on the counter.

"It won't; it's gross," I said, but I went and got it for him anyway.

"You should try new things," Jonathon said, "Dad always said, a change is as good as a rest."

I didn't agree, but I wasn't going to go there. He was probably being sarcastic anyway, in that way of his that I have never understood. I put my hand in Eli's. I wondered if my dad had ever cheated on my mum, or thought of leaving her.

We looked out the window. A small unmanicured garden; a cleared patch with two tree stumps, a circle of tall wildflowers, some paving stones, a compost bin. It had been cold and rainy the previous day but this morning was merely cloudy. Beyond the clearing, acres of trees.

"Are there bears in these here parts?" I asked.

Both Jonathon and Eli mumbled that there probably were.

"Nice windows," Eli said. "Big spacious view. Like we are inside and outside at the same time."

"Yup," Jonathon agreed. He stirred the maple syrup in his coffee. He pushed the can towards me and I pushed it back. "Nobody here for miles."

"Yeah, you shouldn't take it personally that the crowd was so small last night. I mean, nobody lives here," I said. I rose and started washing my cup in the sink. Eli followed me, and waited behind me to wash his. Jonathon stood up too, and walked over to another window.

Suddenly he yelled.

"Look! A bear!"

It was small, black, and alone. I stood close to Jonathon at the window, our noses pressed to the glass like children. We watched, completely fascinated, as it lumbered about slowly in its bearlike way, nose up and wagging as if contemplating the smell of our coffee.

"Is it a cub? It's so small and cute," I said.

Eli hadn't moved from the sink, but he looked across the room. He said he thought it was at least a teenager, that black bears didn't get very big. The bear walked around the patio at the side of the house, approached the front door but then turned back again.

"Wow," said Jonathon. "You were just talking about whether there were bears and look, there's one right there."

"I've never seen one before," he added. "This is my first bear."

I said, "Me neither" and, "Me too".

"He is so cute," I said again.

Eli watched us. "Where I come from, we trap those guys. Or shoot them." He had grown up in Northern Quebec. I tried to get that picture out of my mind, the bear in anguish, in a leg-hold trap, the bear sauntering about innocently and a bullet coming out of nowhere, like in *JFK*, bursting through him and turning his head into gory pulp.

"Maybe I should yell at him to go away," Eli said, but we ignored him.

"Is he looking at us too?" asked Jonathon. "Are we, like, looking at each other through the glass? Does he find us interesting too? Is he thinking, 'Whoa, look at those humans, they're so humanlike, it's incredible.'"

"I feel like I'm watching TV but I am in the show at the same time," I said.

The phone rang. It was Lisa.

"There's a bear," I said as I answered it, instead of, "Good morning."

"Oh, right. Well, just shout out the window and he'll go away."

"What? No! This is a treat for us."

"Oh, okay. Is he in the compost?"

"No."

"So anyway, we were wondering around what time you were heading out."

"Oh, as soon as we stop watching the bear."

I looked at Jonathon as I hung up the phone. His face was flushed, his eyes shining. He looked thirteen, tops. That would make me fifteen, except at fifteen I thought I knew everything.

The bear was in the compost now.

"Bam-Bam's in the compost now," I sang out.

Jonathon glanced at me and he started to smile, the first smile I had seen on his face in ages. He remembered. When things weren't going that well, when he struck out at his first baseball game, when his best friend shared his gum with some other kid, when our parents were angry at us, or worse, at each other, I always made Bam-Bam, Jonathon's teddy bear with the drum strapped around him, come to the rescue. I'd make him fly through the air, land in his mop of curls, tickle him in the stomach.

"Listen, kiddies," Eli said slowly after a few minutes, "I think we should get going. Wasn't Lisa hinting that they're waiting for us?"

"What?"

Eli cleared his throat. "We have to go to the barn and pack up," he said gruffly. He came between us, unlatched the window, and was about to shout but the bear took the hint and scrambled off. It ran in the cutest way. It had a sweet little bum and its legs were impossibly short.

"Bam-Bam had to go," I said to Jonathon, stroking his head.

"Places to go, people to meet," Jonathon said wryly.

"Maybe he had a gig," I said.

"A tickle gig," I added.

Eli waited with diminishing patience at the other end of the house, his hand on the doorknob.

Fruit, Nut, Reality

"Hey, look at that. Wouldn't you like a piece of that?" Sergei made a low whistling sound as Pam from Accounting walked by in a pair of low-cut celery-coloured corduroy pants.

"A piece of what?" said Buddy, not quite looking up. "A piece of pie? I wouldn't say no to a piece of pie, no sirree."

"You are so… how can I say… foreign." Sergei's sigh said even more. *You are pathetic. You are not a man.* Even, *you have no penis.*

Sandra wondered what Buddy thought of being called foreign by the foreigner. Buddy was from a small town in Ontario. His parentage was half British and half Japanese-Canadian. The Japanese part manifested itself in his height (five foot four) and his legs, which were short, even for him. His father had been a fisherman on the west coast. A *tiny* fisherman, he had told Sandra, which made her think of a drawing of a stick figure on an enormous boat, in rocky waters. But Buddy wasn't tiny; in fact, he was pretty fat. Maybe that was his mother's side.

Sandra and Buddy went for walks every day at lunchtime, but nobody ever asked questions about *that*. Buddy was married, for one thing, and Sandra had someone for *that*. People trusted Buddy, felt comfortable with him, maybe because he always seemed so comfortable with himself. He was twenty-nine years old, but, married and a father, could pass for forty-five. He dressed simply but in bright colours, the way an overprotective mother dresses a little boy. He was, Sandra often thought, endearingly young and old at the same time.

Sergei, on the other hand, was somewhere in his mid-thirties, tall and muscular, with big hands and a thick neck. There was nothing remarkable about the way he dressed, apart from the white pants he sometimes wore at office parties—but he had brought a lamp to work one day that seemed to express something about him. It consisted of a pile of splayed white hair-like strands gathered up at one end and stuck in a small white plastic funnel bolted inside an upside-down black saucer, from which the light (of many different hues, from blue-grey to violet) emanated. The saucer sat in a white plastic sombrero-shaped base, supported by three plastic prongs. The hairs waved about a bit as the structure rotated, their tips appearing to be lit. The rotation was accompanied by a great deal of noise, the kind you would associate with a small electrical fan.

"That's one ugly object," Sandra said almost every day.

"You should talk," Sergei would answer automatically.

Buddy would only smile amiably, as if he didn't understand English.

Sergei had arrived from Vladivostok seven years earlier, the male equivalent of a Russian mail-order bride. His wife had been a pathologically shy catalogue artist. Sergei divorced her after obtaining his Canadian citizenship, ostensibly because he had given her a bad back through "too much fuck," ending their sex life, and because he was not meant for monogamy, he said, let alone platonic monogamy.

"I am Tech Support," Sergei was shouting into the phone. "I am not psychiatrist. You call me again for made-up problem, I kick your ass." As he put the phone down he added, "Fucking gay. Next time wanna flirt, I kill you."

Sergei walked over and stood by Buddy's desk. Sandra watched from hers, on the other side of the room.

"You. Why you not tell me Zack is homosexual?"

Buddy continued to look at his computer screen for a moment. Then he said, "Did you ask?"

"No, but you should warn me."

"About what?"

"About homosexual."

"Warn you about homosexual."

"Right!" Sergei turned bright pink. The flush started at his neck and moved up, the colour spreading as if someone had just added a cup of cranberry juice to a tall glass of water.

Later that day, Sandra showed Buddy the note. That childish font, the one he himself used for personal messages. It read, "Sergei is gay! Not that there is anything wrong with that."

"He'll think it's me."

"What? Oh, because of the font. Yeah, maybe. Do you mind?"

"Why would I mind? We know he's perfectly well-balanced, would never dream of physically attacking anyone."

"If you end up in the hospital, I'll bring you blueberry pie."

"Deal." He rubbed his stomach in mock anticipation, and smiled so high up in his cheekbones that his eyes disappeared. "Vanilla ice cream is always a nice touch."

Sandra repressed an urge to kiss Buddy on the cheek. The truth was, she thought, nobody would think the note was from Buddy. Buddy never tried to get under anyone's skin.

Sergei and Buddy carpooled. One day, as Sergei was dropping Buddy off at his suburban home, he noticed an unfamiliar girl playing in the sprinkler with Buddy's son and daughter.

"What, you have three kids now?"

"She's my sister, not a kid."

"But she's a kid, no? How old? Teenager?"

"No," said Buddy evenly.

"Not fat like you."

"No, not fat like me."

Keiko's dark hair was shiny and wet, and fell nearly to her waist like a soft black curtain. She wore a pink bikini. The kids, Lou and Mika, were running in crazed circles around her, spraying her with long green plastic water guns and shrieking with laughter.

"How old?" demanded Sergei.

"Twenty-six. Keiko's twenty-six," Buddy said tensely.

"Twenty-six?" Sergei seemed to be turning the number around and around in his head. "Well, that's old enough. Very nice."

Buddy pressed his lips together as if he was trying to smile, and said nothing as he heaved himself out of Sergei's 1999 Cadillac.

Keiko's arms were bare, revealing glistening skin and a tattoo of a Japanese character on her left shoulder. It meant, she had told Buddy, *fruit, nut* and *reality*.

Buddy noticed that Sergei's Cadillac had not pulled away from the curb yet.

"It means *nut*," he called to him.

"What?"

"The tattoo."

"Oh," Sergei said, and nodded and grinned to himself. "Like tough nut to crack."

Buddy didn't say anything. He walked over to his kids, his hands up in surrender. A moment later, out of the corner of his eye, he saw the Cadillac was now parked across the street, and that Sergei had intercepted Buddy's wife Jeannie as she walked up the street with a bag of groceries. He was now carrying the bag inside the house for her.

Jeannie was serving the pork chops. Keiko sat between the children. She was still in her bathing suit, wearing a towel on her head like someone in an ad for a spa.

"How many, Keiko?"

"That's okay Jeannie. I'll just have applesauce and potatoes."

Jeannie raised an eyebrow.

"You vegetarian again?"

"Uh-huh."

"You don't eat pork chop?" asked Sergei.

"That's right. I don't eat meat."

"Why not?"

The two looked at each other for a long moment.

"She doesn't eat meat," said Lou, his mouth full.

"Like before when she didn't," offered Mika.

"Never?"

"Well, not these days. Not today," said Keiko with uncharacteristic bashfulness.

"Maybe tomorrow?"

"I don't think so." Keiko pulled the towel off her head and shook her dark brown hair around her. It had begun to dry, turning lighter and revealing a golden auburn glow.

"We will see," said Sergei.

Keiko grinned. Something about her face was very childlike. Buddy saw Jeannie wince. He quickly turned to look at his plate and dig into his pork chop before their eyes could meet.

"I heard Sergei stayed for supper at your house last night," Sandra informed Buddy the next morning.

"You heard correct," Buddy said as he settled himself in his chair and turned on the computer.

"How was that?"

"Jeannie stopped at the Supergrocers on her way home from work and she bought all kinds of great food. We had pork chops, mashed blue potatoes, applesauce. Lots of butter on the potatoes. Pistachio ice cream for dessert."

"Sounds good. Heard your sister was there."

"Yup. Keiko lost her job again so we hired her to babysit the kids after school. She usually stays for supper."

178

"And, so, how did that go?"

"Oh, fine. Keiko had way too much applesauce though. Sets a bad example for the kids."

"And Sergei?"

"Oh, I can't remember if he even tried the applesauce."

"Did he behave?"

Buddy gave her his simpleton smile.

"Apparently she made an impression on him, you know," Sandra said.

"I'm getting hungry," announced Buddy. "I wonder if the cafeteria has oatmeal-raisin cookies today."

"So, if Sergei goes out with your sister… "

"That's okay," Buddy said quickly. "I don't even like my sister."

"Buddy, you like everybody."

That was the consensus in the office at least. But maybe it was just that everybody liked Buddy.

It was true. Buddy didn't actually like his sister. If anyone asked about it, he would say something unconvincing about injustices dating back to their teenagehood. Keiko listening to boy bands at ear-splitting levels, Keiko monopolizing the phone, Keiko breaking their parents' hearts.

"Wait, how did she do that?"

"She… she moved out."

"Not exactly the crime of the century."

"She is my sister and she pushes my buttons." Buddy looked at Sandra. *I'm not as mild-mannered as I look.*

When Keiko was sixteen, she fell in love with a skinny loser almost twice her age. He was into vegetarianism and scrounging off other people, as far as Buddy could tell. For some reason, Keiko, still a child, decided she wanted to bear this man's children. To the loser's credit, he did not care for the idea at all. Keiko told Buddy she had a plan: poke holes in the safes. Buddy told her, very matter of fact, that it was time for him to snitch on her. At which point Keiko disappeared. For a full year.

When she resurfaced, she had no child. But she had a tattoo, a life-threatening disease and ambivalent feelings about vegetarianism.

"He's refreshing," Keiko had said to Buddy as Buddy drove her home after the supper with Sergei.

"The lemonade was refreshing. Jeannie makes a mean lemonade."

Keiko went quiet, looking out the window as the tree-lined streets fell out of view, and the landscape turned drier, dustier, and more urban.

"What's going on with your T-cell count?" Buddy asked, in the same tone as he might have asked what Keiko thought of the lemonade.

"Everything's A-OK," Keiko said.

"That's peachy."

There was another silence, and then she said, "There's an Italian AIDS march this weekend."

"An *Italian* AIDS march?"

"Yup. In Little Italy, in, you know, that park in front of the cathedral."

"Oh."

"Do you think I should invite Sergei?"

"Do *you* think you should invite Sergei?" In truth, Buddy was stunned by the question. Why would you invite Sergei? Then he said it out loud.

"Why would you invite Sergei?"

"I... like him?" she said in the *am-I-talking-to-a-retard* tone of their never so distant adolescence.

Buddy pulled up in front of Keiko's three-storey brownstone building. A skinny teenager with a cloud of puffy white hair was dribbling a basketball up and down the sidewalk by himself.

"Hey Q-tip!" Keiko called out cheerily.

Q-tip stopped and grinned shyly at Keiko.

"I think you should invite Q-tip," said Buddy. "Q-tip and his ball. He'd be fun for Lou and Mika."

"So YOU guys are coming?" Keiko threw her arms around her brother. Buddy patted her back awkwardly and then nudged her toward the door.

"Sure. Why not? Park means picnic. Those Italians will know how to put on a good spread."

Buddy tried to remember the last time Keiko had followed his advice about anything. He sat in the car watching Q-tip whiz around Keiko, dribbling his ball. He closed his eyes for a moment and listened to some sparrows and squirrels chirp and chatter at each other. His cell phone buzzed. A text from Sandra, asking what was new. Outside his window, a boy and girl were shouting at each other.

"You are one stupid fuck."

"So, you are like TWO stupid fucks, you fat stupid fuck."

Buddy looked out the window and into his sister's eyes.

"Yeah, why not. Invite the guy."

The Search

Jude awoke with a dull headache, a gluey sensation in the undersides of his lips, and this question: *Where is the car?* It had snowed in the night. He got up, or halfway up, knelt on his bed, and leaned forward, steadying himself with his elbows and forearms against the windowpane in front of him. The cars, like indistinguishable lumpy cakes crudely assembled and iced by young children, sat in a line on the right side of his narrow street. If his car were one of the ones in that line, in this block, he would be all right. Parking was allowed on one side of the street each morning so that the snow ploughs could clear the other. The no-parking thing alternated. But where *was* the car? Wait, what day was it? He had been to a party the night before, and he wasn't sure he'd driven home. The party had been a few blocks away, though he wasn't sure where. He *shouldn't* have driven home, that much was clear. He must have driven *to* the party from the airport where he'd picked up his brother.

Speaking of whom: where was Jeremy? He frowned at the extra blanket and pillow, which lay untouched on the hide-a-bed.

"Jeremy?"

Silence.

Jude rarely used his car, apart from special occasions like picking up his younger brother when he visited, or stocking up on toilet paper and canned tomatoes at Costco, or hauling his bass to his band's infrequent but impressively remote gigs. Because of the latter, he could write off the car as an expense, even if it was hard to justify for any other reason: a 1989 Buick LeSabre, a big creaking hulk of rusting black metal, about as fuel-efficient as a bus. He pulled a pair of blue jeans over his boxers, examined a brown cotton sweater for stains, sniffed its armpits and his own, pulled the sweater over his head, matched two of the socks under his bed, and wondered again vaguely where Jeremy was. He wished he were here, making coffee. Jeremy had better not be expecting *him* to make him coffee whenever he decided to come back.

He pulled on his khaki army-surplus parka, put on his boots and started for the door when he heard his mother's voice telling him to put on a hat and gloves. Well, Mum had died when she was fifty-two, so so much for hats and gloves. He ran down the stairs.

Where's your brother?

I don't know, Mum.

Where is the car?

The car had belonged to his dad, an architect who drank at night, also dead.

That's going to be even harder, Mum.

Outside, he gazed hopelessly at the line of cars. He heard a voice, a real one, call his name. Up a block and a half, across the street.

Jude followed the voice to a laundromat and finally, gazing up, spotted Jeremy on the top floor of the building, leaning out a window, unmistakable with his unfashionably long curly hair and even more unfashionable cigarette dangling from the corner of his mouth. When they were younger, *Jeremy* had looked up to *Jude*. Jeremy observed every unoriginal milestone of Jude's, like learning to make sense of letters or balancing himself on a bicycle seat, as feats of pure magic. Also, their sour-breathed father's rages made Jude the ultimate protector. Some nights, Jeremy would lie crying in bed, soaked in sweat, unable to articulate what was bothering him. Dad would crash into the bedroom, shouting. Mum would be behind him, fretting, trying to appease, but her wide scared eyes, pale cotton nightgown and small bare feet belied her uselessness. Jeremy would wail louder, and Jude would have to get out of his warm bed to calm his brother down.

"Dude," Jude said now, "You spent the night up there?"

"Yup," Jeremy said, grinning.

"Not with a chick."

A pause while Jeremy took his cigarette out of his mouth, quickly took a puff, and exhaled, smiling.

"Come off it, Jeremy. Whose apartment is that?"

"I think, I think… her name is Rita."

"Yeah, right. Where is this chick?"

"Around here. At work. She's a meter maid."

"Whatever."

"No, really. This is, like, her beat, I think they call it. Hey, I think your car got towed away, man."

"Dude! What?"

"Yeah, yeah. She wrote a ticket, put it on your windshield. Hey did you *know* they towed cars here?" He tapped the ashes off his cigarette. Jude ducked as they fell and made a tiny, dark shallow hole in the snow below. His brother's head retreated from the window and in a moment he was downstairs in a parka like Jude's, only blue. Jeremy's eyes were like his too, brown, but like their mother's, flecked with green. Jeremy was exactly half his mother's age when she died. *We'd better hurry; we don't have much time to grow up.*

"You slept with a meter maid?"

"Let's go get a coffee."

Jeremy was obviously enjoying himself, maybe more than he had the night before. Jeremy never put much effort into anything; Jude couldn't see how a guy like that could even enjoy being with a woman that much.

"Isn't a meter maid a kind of cop? What would a cop be doing with a bad boy like you?" Jude glanced at his brother as they began to walk through the snowy streets. *I haven't shaved in a couple of days, but he's going on day six, I bet.*

They came to the corner diner.

"It's kind of pretty, the snow," Jeremy said. He paused at the door and turned and waved his hands around. "It's so magical."

Jude mumbled, "Whatever," again and left his brother to his ges-ticulations outside. He ordered coffee, sat at a table at the front and watched Jeremy through the window. He wondered how much the ticket and the towing would cost. He tried to recall a woman named Rita from the party, but could not remember anything at all. Then in a flash, he remembered leaving, stumbling a bit as he came down a staircase, and being outside the laundromat.

His brother, he realized, had never left the party.

Then more pictures came back. There was no Rita. There had been a bunch of hairy guys, friends of friends of Jeremy that he had made tree-planting out west. There was some beer, some weed, then something else from a Ziploc bag that smelt like a burning shower curtain. Jeremy getting up abruptly, giving him his coat and pushing him out of the room. The slippery staircase, falling out the door, the fresh air on his face.

"Abracadabra!" Jeremy was shouting, his voice only half-muffled by the thick paned window. With a cigarette between his lips, he began drawing letters in the snow piled on the side windows of a parked car.

"Fucker?" Jude read aloud, but then, just as he recognized the stylish curve of the window frames, made out "Sucker." He laughed and pounded on the window. He might leave his car there forever. It wasn't worth the bother.

The Jumpsuit

Well, she swears this never happened.

I wonder where it came from, in the first place. Was I the sort of child who, walking through a store holding her mother's hand, would stop at the sight of a desired object and whine and demand until she acquiesced?

Maybe my father bought it for me. I don't remember if he was there with us at the lake that week. Anyway, he was colour blind, and probably had no opinion about it one way or another.

Where was the lake? Were we at a cottage?

There are parts of my childhood that have faded to wide blank streaks. Irretrievable.

I remember a duffle bag by a cot. In the duffle bag, my mother had packed several changes of clothes for me. My intention was to ignore them all.

What I wore, every single day, over my bathing suit: my awesome, cool, sleeveless lime-green terry-cloth jumpsuit, with the silver zipper down the front. Down went the zip and I'd come out like an animal from its exquisite green shell, splash into the water, out again, step right back inside it, the soft towelly texture of the terry-cloth absorbing the water dripping off my skin. Up went the zip, and I'd be dressed, lime green, cozy again.

Every day. And every day as I came out to the porch for breakfast, my mother would wince. She would talk about how much

186

nicer she found the other clothes I had, how nobody else in the world wore the same thing for days on end, how lime green was an awful colour that made her head hurt behind her eyes.

I didn't see what any of this had to do with me. Every night I'd rinse it out in the bathroom sink. The water there seemed to make it softer. When it dried, I wrapped it around my pillow, rested my cheek on it and went to sleep.

I was seven years old.

I was sitting on the dock, watching butterflies. The sky was powder blue, the sun hot. A shadow fell on the dock in front of me. It was my mother. She seemed nervous and happy. She was laughing girlishly. She had let her curly hair grow past her shoulders, and I thought that she looked beautiful. She asked if I wanted to come out on the boat.

Being on the boat wasn't really my thing. To me, a boat was an annoying barrier between my body and the sparkling, gorgeous water. But having my mother's undivided attention for an hour probably appealed to me. Maybe I was the kind of child who liked to tell stories and jokes and sing silly songs, and have my mother make encouraging listening sounds. I don't remember.

But I do remember that as my mother rowed toward the center of the lake, I began to regret having come. Somehow there was nothing much to talk about. It was too hot. The sun beat down cruelly. A few grey clouds had formed, but there was no real sign of rain.

Although my mother was doing all the rowing, she seemed cool in her black and white bathing suit. She wore huge, black sunglasses like Jackie Onassis. She smiled at me.

"I'm hot," I whimpered.

"Yes, it must be hot in that suit."

"It's okay," I said. Despite the heat, I felt a chill on the back of my neck.

"Why don't you go for a swim?" she asked brightly.

"That's okay," I said.

187

Suddenly she stopped rowing. She had evidently found what she was looking for, the place directly under the sun. She leaned back and turned her face up. I wondered if her sunglasses helped deflect the heat. Her skin merely shone a little bit, while mine was dripping with sweat.

"It must be hot in that jumpsuit," she insisted.

I zipped out of my suit and then sat down on it, looking glumly at the water.

"Are we going back soon or are we just going to sit here?"

My mother never stopped smiling. I wished I could see her eyes.

"I don't know," she answered dreamily. "I'm tired of rowing. I thought we'd just enjoy the sun for a little while."

The air, the sky, the sun were oppressively white-hot. Sweat was pouring from me. The lake, like a giant vat of iced tea, was making me thirsty. My mother, the corners of her mouth still turned up, put down her oars, leaned back, and started to breathe with heavy, even little rasps.

I stood up a little shakily, and tried to look under her sunglasses.

"Mummy?" I whispered.

No answer.

"Mummy? I'm going for a swim."

I glanced at my jumpsuit, folded neatly on my seat. I fished a towel out of my mother's wicker bag and placed it on top.

In I went. The water was not as cool as I had expected. There was no relief to be had as I darted around in the warm water. The sun slapped my face and burned my eyes every time I came up for air.

When I climbed back into the boat my heart was beating wildly. My mother looked even more serene and beautiful. I grabbed the towel off the seat. The seat was bare.

"Where is it?" I screamed.

"Where's what, sweetie?" my mother asked. Her smile was sweet and frightening at the same time.

"Where's my jumpsuit?"

"I don't know. Where'd you put it?"

I didn't bother searching her bag. I didn't say a word on the way back. My mother, I seem to recall, hummed to herself a little.

With Friends Like These

I looked everywhere for her, for years. I had no contacts, no traces, but nevertheless checked every face in every crowd, on every bus, in every audience at any show I happened to attend. I walked around her old working-class neighbourhood, which had morphed into the Gay Village. I awoke from dreams of emptying my pockets and finding a small gleaming gem, or of discovering a new room in my house, a room bathed in sunlight, knowing the dream was really about Anne-Marie.

I am going to tell you about the worst thing I have ever done. I know it was wrong now, but didn't then because it was back when the baby boomers, especially the ones about ten years older than me, were still young. They were remaking the world. They were remaking *morality*. And they held me in their thrall.

Well, one of them did, anyway. His name was Denis, and he liked young girls. These feelings, combined with the *air du temps*, gave him a particular worldview that had implications for our relationship and for my relationships with other people.

The fact that Denis was twenty-seven and interested in me, a seventeen-year-old who looked even younger, should have struck me as weird, but all I really felt was flattered. I had run away from home, but in a dutiful-daughter kind of way. I continued going to school, and even told my parents where I lived. I just hadn't warned them before I left that I was saving up all my babysitting money and had a suitcase waiting in my closet for the day that I could escape the insanity of living with them. I saw my parents as clued-out immigrants. I loathed my father, a schizophrenic who was more tuned in to the voices in his own head than he was to the people in his life. He snapped out of his delusional state occasionally to dole out slaps when I wasn't "obedient." I can hear the snarkiness in my tone here, the voice of my awful teenage self. I hadn't learned to be sympathetic to my parents yet.

That winter, I moved into an apartment on Marquette Street that Denis had begun to renovate and decorate in the hippie style that I adored. Braided rugs, pine floors, a tangle of plants on swinging shelves he had built for them. I helped him strip the paint off all the wood cabinets and door and window frames. It was a three-and-a-half, and the only real bedroom was supposed to be mine, but soon after I moved in we began to share his futon in the living room. We would prepare gourmet meals together, drink red wine, listen to music. He introduced me to Jacques Brel, Georges Brassens, and Serge Gainsbourg, his idol. He had long hair and a beard that made him look vaguely feral. He sometimes wore a poncho. He played the guitar, was a polyglot; in fact, he was learning to speak Mandarin. I thought he was the coolest person I had ever met. He had a lot of different cameras, and he liked to take black-and-white pictures of me and develop them in his darkroom. He emulated another idol of his, the photographer David Hamilton, who also took pictures of young girls. Once a week, he would receive large manila envelopes with the name of an American summer camp in the upper left-hand corner. After a while, I realized that the contents consisted of copies of a magazine filled with photos of children vacationing with their families at a nudist camp. It didn't strike me as odd. It didn't strike me as anything at the time.

But a few months later, after my eighteenth birthday, he began to turn away from me in bed. One bright afternoon I cornered him and forced him to confess his problem. He told me his tragic story:

he was still in love with his first crush, his childhood sweetheart. She was his cousin, and they had both been twelve at the time. He said he seemed to have gotten stuck there, with her, and could never be attracted to a grown woman. He also consoled me by saying something that now I wish I hadn't accepted as the truth: that all men went off their girlfriends after a few months, and that it was normal. And he said that I should sleep with other men, as many men as I could find. That was normal too. Everything else, he said, was hypocrisy.

"But what about you?" I asked, concerned. After all, he couldn't very well have sex with a twelve-year-old.

"Don't worry about me," he said. This struck me as brave and selfless.

My mother was in denial about the extent of my father's mental illness and its effect on our family. I'm sure it helped her cope, but it was hard for me; I was forced to live in this fantasy where all was well and normal. I had some friends my own age but, looking back, I realize they were fucked up too. There was Zoé, who was overweight, depressed, and in love with both of us. She would come over, say very little, but just not go home, sleeping at the foot of our futon like a dog. There was Jade, who looked like a Rastafarian, but sort of faded like her soft cotton pants, and who at nineteen was already a divorced mother of two. There was Katherine, who was going out with a gay guy, but despite that apparently futile pursuit, always seemed to have profound insights about the people around us. And there was Katherine's friend, Anne-Marie, who became my friend too.

Anne-Marie was the one I betrayed. She was tall and shapely, with huge brown eyes. She had been kicked out of French school by the nuns for having mono. I hadn't been allowed to go to French school because my parents were Hindus. You had to be Catholic and chaste to go to French school in those days. Anne-Marie had arrived in her English high school in the middle of her second-to-last year, understanding very little of what people were saying to her besides "the new frog." When she told me that story, I knew she could understand me better than I understood myself, all without asking any questions. I confessed to her one day, passing her joint back to her, that I thought she was "everything". She laughed and demanded to know why. I made a list and read it to her: she had the long dark hair, sharp features and strong quiet presence of a native; she rode a motorcycle; she was fun, beautiful and fearless. I asked her about boyfriends, and she said she was a virgin. Denis would have said, "What a waste," and because I knew he would have said that, I decided that was my point of view too. Especially after she startled me one afternoon by putting her arm around me as we walked in Parc Lafontaine. I pulled away, but had no answer for her when she asked me why.

I decided my answer was to fix her up with Sean, Jade's ex-husband. I was sure they would get along. They wore the same leather bracelets, love beads, and Peruvian sweaters. They both liked the same bands, the Rolling Stones and the Doors. And they both talked about drugs but never took their experimentation very far. Actually, they were a lot like me. I didn't think Jade would mind. After all, she said she couldn't stand Sean.

One Thursday night a couple of months later, I dropped by Jade's place, but she was out and Sean was looking after the kids, who were sleeping. He told me that he had no idea when she was coming back, that she seemed pissed off about something. I asked him how it was going with Anne-Marie. It was rare that I ever saw one of them without the other anymore. The three of us went dancing at Café Campus every Friday night, where we'd ask the DJ to play the Rolling Stones and the Doors, and he'd always oblige. Sean looked at me through his long strawberry-blond bangs with his big pale eyes and told me that Anne-Marie refused to sleep with him. He looked at me as if I should feel responsible for this turn of events, and I did. I offered to sleep with him.

193

When Jade came home, she recognized my bicycle on the landing, realized Sean and I were in her bedroom, and got pissed off all over again. I didn't understand what all the fuss was about. The next evening, Sean, Anne-Marie and I went to Café Campus, and after a pint or two, Sean and I told Anne-Marie that we had slept together. Because we thought that that is what you had to do. You had to be honest.

I will never forget the look on her face, the bewilderment and the pain, those huge brown eyes. Although this seems incredible to me now, I had to be told why she was sad. It had to be explained to me. "Why am I sad? Because my two closest friends cheated on me. How could you guys do that to me?"

Looking back, it was around then that I first began to realize that Denis's whole way of looking at sex, everybody just loving each other, really seemed to end in a lot of hurt. Denis hurt me. I hurt Anne-Marie. Even Sean was hurt; his reasons seemed more vague at the time, but he really was suffering from a basic lack of love and respect too.

It didn't stop me, though. I followed Denis's advice and began travelling: backpacking around, sleeping around too, because this was the only thing that seemed to relieve my feelings of rejection by him. After coming home, I started university and saw Anne-Marie once in awhile, but we were both busy. Several years went by, and I received a phone call from a man I didn't know.

He said he was Anne-Marie's boyfriend, Marc.

"Oh, that's... that's great," I said. *Why was that great?* By then, I knew something about homosexuality, wasn't ready to just dismiss it as an error or the result of sexual inexperience.

"I'm planning a surprise birthday party for Anne-Marie and I found your number in her address book." He seemed delighted with himself.

"Sure," I said. "I'll come."

Anne-Marie and Marc lived in a modern high-rise on Guy Street downtown. The furniture, walls, and rugs were all different shades of beige. People stood around with drinks in their hands like at one of my mother's faculty parties. There was no dancing, just dull small talk. When I first entered the apartment, I didn't see Anne-Marie. Then I realized she was watching me apprehensively from the opposite side of the room. I nearly jumped. What I had been hoping to find: Anne-Marie, still a hippie, maybe dressed with a little bisexual edge now. Instead, she dressed like the adult I had yet to become. Her hair was cut in a bob, and she wore make-up and a dress that fit her properly, instead of loose Indian shirts and sloppy jeans.

Finally, she crossed the room. We kissed each other politely. She didn't smell of Patchouli anymore. I wished her a happy birthday and she told me she hadn't been expecting me.

"Yeah, I know. Surprise!"

"Marc went through my address book," she said, almost apologetically.

"He seems great," I said without a trace of sincerity. He seems boring, is what I wanted to say. He had short dark hair and was wearing a suit. I smirked to myself as I thought about how surprised he must have been when he opened the door and saw that I wasn't white.

"How is university?" she asked.

"It's interesting. What are you up to?"

"I got a job working as a nurse's aide in a psychiatric hospital."

"Really? How is that?" I was appalled. At the same time, I guessed a steady job would pay better than the part-time jobs I took as a student. Hence the clean beige apartment.

"It's draining," Anne-Marie said slowly, gazing to her left as she chose her words, "but it's very rewarding, very emotionally fulfilling." She didn't bother to elaborate. She seemed suddenly tired of our conversation. Her eyes met mine, though, and rested there for an uncomfortable moment. I think they said: *you could never understand.*

I don't remember much else about that night. I remember running into Katherine a few days later, and that she asked me about the party that she had missed.

"Oh, I was so disappointed," I said. "She's so straight now. She looks like a secretary."

That was all I had to say about someone who had been a good friend.

I ran into Katherine again later that month, and she told me that Anne-Marie was hurt by what I'd said. Once again, I had no clue what I had done wrong.

"Well," Katherine said, " she said, 'What, I'm not allowed to change? Just because I change my clothes, she doesn't like me anymore?'"

"I just think… " I said, with the sort of certainty you have when you are young, "I think clothes can say a lot about who you are. I think her clothes say she's really conventional now."

A few years later I got married, and a few years after that a woman I knew whose kids played with mine had an affair with my husband. I can't say that she was a friend of mine; she wasn't. She was sneaky and manipulative, aware of what she was doing. When I slept with Sean, I was just a dumb kid. But the thing is, only when it happened to me did I realize how horribly painful it was. I could barely function. It was suddenly almost impossible to hear anyone properly, to focus on anything, to eat or sleep. That's when I began looking for Anne-Marie, wanting to acknowledge the pain I had caused her and to finally apologize.

Three years ago, my teenage daughter found her for me on Facebook. Anne-Marie's hair was cut shorter, her features more defined, and she was playing the tuba, an instrument I had recently taken up. Excited, I sent her a message through my daughter's

Facebook account. She answered a few months later, apologized politely for the delay, said she had just come back from Europe. She said her own daughter had set up the Facebook account for her.

I quickly replied, asking her to call or e-mail me.

But that was all. I never heard from her again.

My daughter sent her a message inviting her to a surprise birthday party for me. She noted the tuba coincidence. Anne-Marie never answered.

I got on Facebook myself and tried to friend her. She ignored the request.

Suddenly, a few weeks ago, I got a message saying she had accepted my friend request. I eagerly went on her Facebook page, looked at pictures of her, her beautiful daughter, and her husband, a guy with longish white hair. In some pictures, they were all playing music together. I sent her another message, this time a heartfelt apology, and mentioned that I thought she had a lovely family. There was no reply. Last week, she changed her status from "married" to "single." I found out when I went on her page to spy on her. I had heard that people did that; that was the reason for my reluctance to get on Facebook in the first place. The idea that some creepy ex-friends or ex-lovers would be watching my life unfold. It even struck me that Denis might want to see pictures of my children. God knows where he is now, what he has done.

But it was explained to me that if you didn't friend someone, they couldn't do that.

Which leads to the question: why did Anne-Marie friend me? Can I ask her that?

And how would I put it? Would I say, "Why on earth would you want to be my friend?"

Yes, I think that is how I would put it.

ESPLANADE
Books
THE FICTION SERIES AT VÉHICULE PRESS

Véhicule Press

Acknowledgements

I would like to thank my editor, Dimitri Nasrallah, as well as my mentors Dennis Bock, of the Humber School for Writers, and Elise Moser.

I wrote these stories over several years and would have quit several times had it not been for the patience, encouragement and excellent advice of Guillaume Bourque, Annick Corbeil, Sandra Edmunds, Joe and Saskia Ferrar, Christine Finlayson, Erin Fitzgerald, Julie Frédette, Frédéric Samson, Daniel Sanger, Joan Sutton Strauss, Deborah Sutton, Cary Tennis, and Suzanne Walsh.

I would also like to thank the following editors for publishing earlier versions of some of these stories: Billy Fontenot, of the *Louisiana Review*; Benjamin Wachs, of *Fiction 365*; and William Males, of *Frostwriting*.

"What I Really Did" appeaed in the anthology *Salut King Kong: New English Writing from Quebec* (Véhicule Press). "Fruit, Nut, Reality," "Something Steady" and "The Perfect Guy" first appeared on Fiction365.com. An earlier version of "Indelible Markers" and "Elephant Heart" appeared in *The Louisiana Review*. Parts of "Indelible Markers," as it appears in this collection, were published as "Greek Story" on Frostwriting.com.